UNTIMELY DEPARTURE

MYSTIC INN MYSTERIES

STEPHANIE DAMORE

ONE

Chestnuts roasting on an open fire;
The Wicked Witch cursing off your nose.
Hexes and spells being sung by the choir,
With bubbling potions that warm your toes.

I hummed along with the tune while adding a strand of red tinsel to the lobby's Christmas tree. From behind me, even Percy was in a festive spirit. The poltergeist straightened his green plaid bow tie in the reception area's mirror before eying his combed-over hairstyle. I watched as he carefully smoothed a stray hair back into place.

"You're looking dapper. Eleanor coming home today?" I turned back to the tree and continued decorating.

"All the way from Surrey." Percy's ghost of a girlfriend, who we had recently freed from a two-hundred-year imprisonment, had spent the remainder of the fall visiting with her sister who haunted a lovely cottage in Southeast England. It was cute how smitten our poltergeist was with the ghost. And for not the first time, I was grateful he had someone to occupy his thoughts and keep him out of trouble—or mostly out of trouble. A poltergeist was still a poltergeist after all.

I was about to ask Percy what his plans were for the day, because surely he had something sweet planned for Eleanor's first day home, when my cell phone rang in my back pocket. I let the strand of red tinsel dangle from the tree branch as I slid my phone out of my jeans.

It was Aunt Thelma.

She and her best friend Clemmie were setting up their table at the craft show at the high school. The craft show, along with a silent auction and bake sale, were all part of the fundraising effort to win the Witch News Network's Christmas Wish Contest. The network used the money to grant Christmas wishes to witches all around the world, and the town that raised the most money won a glittering New Year's Eve ball complete with live music and entertainment. Mayor Parrish was adamant that this would be Silverlake's year to win it, and she planned on announcing the results at the Christmas tree lighting ceremony Monday evening. Rumor had it, she'd already picked out her evening gown and was planning on following up the ball with a New Year's Day brunch. I had to hand it to the woman, she was ambitious.

Before I could even get the word hello out, Aunt Thelma started talking.

"Angelica? Can you hear me?"

"I can hear you."

"Good, you need to get down here right away. It's an emergency!"

I backed away from the tree and turned around to face Percy.

His eyes locked with mine. "What's wrong?" he asked, picking up on my alarmed expression.

I asked Aunt Thelma the same question.

"It's Mrs. Potts's cat. He ran off with half our inventory. We need more feathers!" Aunt Thelma answered in a huff.

"And a hot glue gun, stat!" Clemmie hollered in the background.

I closed my eyes and let out a sigh, putting my hand on my heart, which was beating rapidly in my chest. "You scared me for a minute. I thought something was really wrong."

"What do you mean? Something is really wrong. Didn't you hear me? Mr. Whiskers has our earrings. We need your help. Clemmie's trying to get them back, but that darn cat crunched them all up. No one is going to buy earrings slicked with slobber."

I scrunched up my face at the mental image. However, Aunt Thelma was right. I knew I wouldn't buy them. I glanced down at my watch. It was just after six-thirty in the evening. Most of the shops in Village Square closed at nine o'clock on weeknights, and seeing tonight was Friday, that meant the craft store would be open for a few more hours.

"Okay, I'll be there as soon as I can. Text me a list of what you need, and I'll drop it off." I'd planned on coming into town to pick Aunt Thelma up anyway. It looked like I'd be making the trip a couple of hours early.

I hung up with Aunt Thelma and gazed lovingly at the half-decorated Christmas tree before tucking the rest of the garland around the backside of the tree and leaving it for later. As much as I wanted to finish decorating, it was going to have to wait.

I left Percy to hold down the fort, took Aunt

Thelma's car keys, and made the quick drive into town. Village Square was the touristy area of Silverlake, and this time of year, it was packed with holiday shoppers. After Thanksgiving, the town council had spent the weekend decorating the winding drive into downtown and the surrounding shops for the holiday season. Volunteers strung multicolored twinkling lights around every pecan tree and replaced the yellow and gold potted mums with bright red poinsettias along the way. Local children were encouraged to add ornaments to the pine trees at Wishing Well Park, and someone had even placed a Santa hat on top of the witch statue that stood in the center of the fountain. We might not see a white Christmas in Silverlake, but that didn't mean it wouldn't still be beautiful.

I waved at my friend Misty as I drove past the bookstore, looking for a place to park. She stood outside, adjusting an evergreen wreath on her shop's door, but still managed to wave back.

Village Square was full of all sorts of curio shops. You could pick up potion ingredients, custom jewelry, specialized herbal teas, a one-of-a-kind wand, not to mention the delicious treats at the candy shop, a hearty meal at the diner, or a tall pint at the tavern. The sight of holiday shoppers filling the cobblestone paths filled me with even more holiday cheer, even if their presence meant a good parking spot was impossible to find. For not the first time, I had assumed it would be faster to drive over when in reality, I might've been quicker taking the Enchanted Trail over to the shops, getting what I needed, and then hightailing it back to the inn and driving to the other side of the lake to the high school. But darn it, it was chilly out, and the sun would be setting soon enough, and the Enchanted Trail and I didn't mix at night, or sometimes not even during the day.

I ended up parking in no man's land, in the back corner parking lot. One more space over, and I'd have parked in the grass. I got out of the car, turned my collar up to the wind, tucked my hand into my fleece, and power walked to the craft shop.

TWO

Thirty minutes later, after running into everyone and anyone in Village Square, I had my shopping bags in hand and was ready to hike back to the car. Surprisingly, Aunt Thelma hadn't called yet and asked where I was, or maybe I just hadn't heard her call over the Christmas music piped over Village Square's outdoor speakers.

The crowds had begun to thin out a bit as the dinner hour wore on. I imagined the diner, tavern, and probably even the Simmering Spoon would be packed. It was a good thing Vance had made reservations for the two of us tomorrow night, or I doubt we'd find a table. I smiled at his thoughtfulness. While I was grateful for the holiday visitors and the inn being busy, all the guests meant more work and less time to spend together. I knew I wasn't the only one feeling the crunch. All my friends were running this way and that way, making sure everyone's holiday was merry and bright. It was exhausting. I was looking forward to slowing things down tomorrow night.

It was at that moment, with my arms full and my mind wrapped up in my thoughts, when my witchy instincts went on high alert. My pace faltered as I looked over my shoulder, expecting to find someone walking up behind me, but instead, the cold wind greeted me with a blast of arctic air. I tucked my chin down and picked up the pace. I was deep within Village Square, and as tempting as it was to dash inside a shop until the feeling passed, I decided to press forward and get to my car as quickly as possible. The sooner I got to Aunt Thelma, the sooner I could get back trimming the Christmas tree and singing carols alongside the fire, which sounded perfect right about then. My toes were turning as frosty as my nose.

I was so focused on my surroundings that I almost walked right into Luke, the candy maker. He outstretched his arms and prevented me from colliding right into him.

"Oh my gosh, sorry," I said with a shocked expression.

"Is everything okay?" Luke looked at me with concern in his eyes.

"Yeah, I just thought I heard something. Sorry, I wasn't paying attention." I cleared my throat and changed the subject. "Are you doing some holiday shopping?" Luke's hands were full of bags from the village shops as well.

"Trying to. I have no idea what to buy the twins this year. And Sally is never any help. She says she doesn't need anything." Sally was Luke's sister, and the twins were his nieces.

I thought back to the shop windows I had passed. "Well, I saw that the toy shop had some pretty believable fake wands in the front window." I raised my eyebrows knowingly. Beatrice and Sabrina were known for playing tricks on one another, or anyone for that matter. "And you can never go wrong with one of Connie's relaxation potions." Some witches liked to take bubble baths or naps to help recharge. Personally, I swore by Connie's relaxation tonic. Somehow, the magic potion knew just what your body needed, and it left you feeling completely blissful.

"You're a genius. Thank you." Luke looked down at his watch.

"You still have time. And you're welcome." I parted ways with Luke and continued to walk to my car, feeling a bit more relaxed and not quite so on edge.

And that's when I felt the man's cold fingertips grip my wrist. I had no idea where he'd come from. One moment I was alone, and next, he was there.

I screamed and yanked my arm back in reflex. It was then, as I was attempting to free myself, that I looked up and realized that I knew the man.

"Sorry, Ange didn't mean to scare you." The man dropped my wrist.

"Daniel? Oh, my goodness, is that you?"

"In the flesh," Daniel smirked.

"You scared the bejesus out of me." I swatted my high school friend on the shoulder. It had been ages since I'd seen him last. Fifteen years at least. Daniel looked as charming as ever with his dark hair, warm eyes, and dimples. He'd be a ringer for Prince Charming if it weren't for all the tattoos, which I happened to know fit his rockstar personality to a T.

Much like the perfectly sculpted t-shirt he wore. Wasn't he cold? I tucked my hands in the front pocket of my fleece, shopping bags dangling from my wrist.

Daniel grinned, and it was then, when he smiled, that I noticed the tips of his canines. Make that fangs. Long, sharp fangs.

I gulped.

"Um...ah..." I stammered at a loss for words.

"It's okay. You can say it." Daniel's manner was nonchalant, but he wasn't fooling anyone. His eyes searched my face as he scrutinized my expression.

"You're a...um...eh..." Despite Daniel's insistence, I couldn't say it. He was wrong. I couldn't believe it, let alone say it.

"I'm a vampire."

"Right. That's the word." I exhaled and looked away, feeling embarrassed. Vampires usually avoided Silverlake, preferring to stay with their kind, but Daniel was first a witch, which explained how he even knew about Silverlake. "I'm sorry. You just surprised me. I hadn't heard."

"You're not the only one. That's why I'm here. Have you seen my gran? I thought she'd be over here shopping, picking up some new yarn or something."

"That's right, she does like to knit, doesn't she." Minerva had a wonderful sense of humor too, knitting the most deliciously awful Christmas sweaters and wearing them with pride.

"Always." Daniel smiled, and this time it was genuine. "Anyway, it didn't feel right sitting outside her house waiting for her to show." Daniel glanced uncomfortably around him. People had already realized what he was and were giving us a wide berth.

I smiled softly, feeling sorry for my friend. "I think I might know where she is. There's a craft show at the high school this weekend. She's probably setting up a table along with everyone else. I'm headed over there now. Do you want a ride?"

"Nah, that's okay. I got my bike. See you there?" Daniel motioned to where his motorcycle stood parked right up in front. Illegally, I might add.

"Sure thing. I parked in the back forty, though, so it'll take me a bit to get there."

"I'll walk you to your car." It was a statement, not a question.

I started to protest, but I didn't want Daniel to think my objection was because he was a vampire. Truthfully though, I was a bit nervous. Maybe it was because of the whole dead aspect or the blood and the fangs part, but vampires always put me on edge. They were powerful and deadly, and if I felt inept at handling a rogue witch, well, it was nothing to how I felt facing a vampire.

But then I remembered that this was Daniel, and he was here to see his grandmother, not only that, but he was a longtime friend. Vampire or not, he wasn't about to rip my throat out in the middle of Village Square. Which was why I found myself saying, "Sure, that would be nice," even if my pulse was a little erratic and my breathing felt shaky.

My thoughts raced as I tried to calm my nerves and come up with an appropriate topic of conversation as we continued our walk.

Daniel beat me to it, "How long have you been back? Last I heard, you were up in Chicago," he asked casually.

"Not long, about six months. My aunt tricked me into coming home." I raised my eyebrows for emphasis.

Daniel shook his head with amusement. "I've always liked Thelma. She goes against the flow, you know?"

I knew exactly what Daniel meant. Aunt Thelma wasn't afraid to be herself. She had a unique sense of style, and she spoke her mind, standing up for her friends and family along the way. I was coming to realize how much I respected her for that and how much I was still trying to find my way in that regard.

"What about you? Are you still playing?" Daniel had hit it somewhat big as a musician, touring the supernatural circuit with his rock band.

"Yeah, up until last week." Daniel left it at that, and I didn't push him, sensing that he didn't want to talk about it.

"Well, I'm sure Minerva will be happy to see you."

Daniel looked at me dubiously. And I looked away.

"Maybe," he said into the nighttime air. "I guess we'll find out."

Five minutes later, I was driving around the lake when my cell phone rang. I barely heard the sound vibrate from the bottom of my purse. Behind me, the steady roar of Daniel's motorcycle reached my car as he quickly caught up.

"What's this about a vampire? Are you okay?" It was Vance.

"Hi, nice to hear from you too." I laughed at how quickly news traveled in our small town. "Who called you?"

"You mean who called me first," Vance clarified.

"There was more than one person?"

"What can I say, people care about you."

"It was Misty, wasn't it?" My eyes flicked to my rearview mirror. Daniel was still behind me.

"One of them, yeah. She couldn't make out who it was but assumed it was a vampire given how fast he got to you. She couldn't hex him fast enough."

"She wouldn't once she saw who it was," I mumbled. Misty had had a mad crush on Daniel back in high school. Well, her and ninety percent of the rest of the school.

"And then Boyd called," Vance continued, not picking up on my comment.

"Boyd?" Boyd was a recently retired lawyer. I was surprised when I found out that the older gentleman was hanging up his bowtie and suspenders. I thought Boyd was going to keep practicing until the day he died. "I didn't even see him."

"He saw you, said a vampire grabbed you. Now, what's going on? Are you okay?"

"I'm fine. The vampire's Daniel. He walked me to my car."

"Daniel McEwen?"

"The one and only. I ran into him at Village Square while picking up some craft supplies for Aunt Thelma. Daniel's in town looking for his grandmother. I told him Minerva was probably at the high school setting up for the craft show. He's following me there now." We stopped at the single red light in town. Daniel's motorcycle slowed to a rumble behind me.

"I didn't even know he was a vampire."

"I know, me either. To tell you the truth, he did scare me. I didn't see him either. But, I'm okay now," I quickly clarified lest Vance felt the need to say something to Daniel. It turned out my witchy instincts had been on point, picking up on Daniel before he reached me. Of course, I hadn't listened to them. I was still learning in that regard.

"Well, if he does attack, don't forget diafotízo."

The spell rolled around on my tongue. "An illumination spell."

"That's the one."

Unlike popular myth, sunlight didn't kill vampires, but it did weaken them, which was why you didn't find many of them walking around on bright sunny days. Instead, they preferred to come out at night when they were at their strongest.

"Honestly, I'm not worried about it now." Or, mostly not, I thought to myself.

"Did he say how long since he was turned?"

"No, he didn't, and it seemed rude to ask," I said as I navigated the turn. "Why?" I felt like there was more Vance wasn't telling me.

Vance hesitated.

"Vance? Don't leave me in the dark here."

"No, you're right. Hopefully, it's nothing. It's just, vampires are strongest right after they're turned. Blood lust and all that."

"Oh gross." On second thought, maybe I didn't want to know. Besides, it could've been months since Daniel had been changed, maybe even years if he avoided coming back home for as long as I did.

"I know. Please be safe."

"I will be, promise." I glanced in my mirror again and hoped I wasn't making a huge mistake having Daniel follow me.

"What time are you done?"

Vance let out a puff of air. "I'm stuck here a couple more hours at least. Call me when you're home?"

"Yeah. Don't work too hard."

"Ha," Vance chuckled as if saying he wished he didn't have to, and I realized how swamped he must be. Vance needed a night off as much as I did.

"Talk soon," I replied as we hung up with one another. I tossed my cell phone on the passenger seat. Yep, tomorrow night couldn't come soon enough.

THREE

I pulled into the gym parking lot, and Daniel parked beside me. He stepped off his motorcycle and waited for me to join him. If all the tourists were at Village Square, then all the locals were at the high school. It reminded me of a Friday night basketball game with how packed the parking lot was. Crafters walked to and from their vehicles, carrying boxes and bins of their wares. Others stood around, socializing with long-time friends. The air was nippy, but that didn't seem to stop people from taking a moment to stop and say hello. It probably helped that the concession stands inside were open, and there was plenty of hot coffee and cocoa to go around.

Although, the moment people spotted Daniel,

coffee and conversation was the farthest thing on people's minds. A hush moved through the crowd. People's sentences faltered as they turned to look as we approached the gymnasium. I couldn't imagine if this was how Daniel felt all the time. It was awful. It was as if people were accusing him of being a criminal just because of what he was. I looked at Daniel out of the corner of my eye. I hadn't meant for him to catch me, but he did.

"Sorry." I wasn't sure if I was apologizing for staring or for people's reactions. Probably both.

"It's alright. Not your fault." Daniel winked and smiled, displaying that rockstar charm he was famous for. But the smile didn't reach his eyes, and I knew it bothered him more than he'd ever admit.

I then thought of something. "This might not be the best place for a reunion." Minerva was going to be surprised, to say the least. Some privacy might be in order.

Daniel slowed his pace. "You're right. You mind going in and seeing if she's here?"

"Not at all. How about you wait in the hallway, by the trophy case?" The hallway trophy case had been in the same place for the last fifty years as far as I knew. It was an easy place to meet up, and it was off to the side, not wide open where people could gawk.

Daniel and I parted ways after walking

through the school's front door, and I headed for the craft show. The buzz and excitement were evident from the moment I stepped through the gym's double doors. Row after row of tables filled the cavernous space, creating a maze of brightly colored crafts. Scanning the room, I spotted dozens of booths I would typically love to stop by. Handmade soaps and lotions, velvet cloaks, down-filled quilts, and crystal jewelry all called to me. But first, I had to drop off the supplies to Aunt Thelma and locate Minerva.

"There you are. I was getting worried about you." Aunt Thelma took plastic bags from my hand and opened them to peer inside.

"What took you so long?" Clemmie stood and looked over my aunt's shoulder.

"It's a long story. Do you know where Minerva is?"

"I think she's right over there, about two rows over, setting up her table." Aunt Thelma pointed with her teal-painted fingernail in the general direction.

"What do you need with Minerva?" Clemmie asked, shifting her attention my way. She wasn't about to let me go with a vague explanation. I decided then and there that I might as well tell them about Daniel. They'd hear about it soon enough based upon the sound of the whispers circulating the gym. In less than two minutes, everyone would know Daniel was a vampire. I quickly recapped my run-in at the Village Square.

"A vampire? Oh, my word." Aunt Thelma looked concerned. From beside her, Clemmie crossed herself. "Poor Minerva, that's going to break her heart."

I looked uneasy. I was afraid of that, as I knew Daniel was.

"Break her heart? We better hope no one stakes his heart." Clemmie eyed Mike Mc-Cormick's woodworking table.

I cringed. Witches did not like vampires.

"No one would do such a thing. We all just need to keep a level head and let the poor boy see his grandmother in peace."

"Which means I better go find her." I wanted to give Silverlake residents the benefit of the doubt, but I couldn't deny how prejudiced witches were against vampires. The sooner Daniel talked to his grandmother, the better.

I excused myself from Aunt Thelma and Clemmie and snaked my way over to where my aunt had pointed, smiling politely and saying hello to locals along the way. But even I got a few side-eyed glances along the way. It hadn't escaped people's attention that I'd arrived with Daniel.

Thankfully, Minerva was where Aunt

Thelma had directed me, and I located her quickly.

I came around the side of the table and moved close so that only Minerva could hear me.

She seemed surprised. "Oh, hello, Angelica. What can I do for you?" She tilted her head in interest.

I leaned forward. "Your grandson, Daniel, is here. He's out by the trophy case, and he wants to speak with you."

"Daniel? He's here? Well now that is a surprise." Minerva's face lit up as if it were Christmas morning. She quickly scooted her chair back and stood, all four and a half feet of her. Part of me felt like I should give her a heads up, but I wasn't sure how to say it. I ended up saying, "It was good to see him. Even if he does seem a bit different."

"Different?" Minerva tilted her head once more as she walked around the table. "Don't tell me he's got more tattoos. The last time I saw him, his arms were covered." Minerva motioned with her fingertips up and down her forearms.

"Not exactly, but he's not the same. I don't want you to be shocked." At that point, I should've come right out and said it. And maybe I would have if we hadn't stepped out into the hallway and right into trouble. Daniel was exactly where he said he would be. He was leaning beside the trophy case, his thumbs hooked in his jeans pockets, glaring down at the petite brunette shaking her finger in his face. I recognized Lorraine Abbott, the high school music teacher, in an instant. And boy was she hot.

"A vampire? You disgust me! Throwing your life away and all your musical talent. What in the world is wrong with you?"

"Will you let me talk?" Daniel managed to get out, but his request fell on deaf ears.

"How dare you step foot in this high school and pollute it with your bloodthirst and your fangs. You don't belong here. I'm going to speak with the town council this instant." Lorraine thrust her finger toward the floor and stomped her foot. "I'll have you thrown out of town before the night is through. Mark my words."

"And here I thought you'd be happy to see me," Daniel drawled.

Lorraine scowled. "You should save us the trouble and get out of town right now. You don't belong here. Not anymore."

I stumbled backward at the music teacher's vitriol.

"Lorraine? What's going on here?" Minerva walked forward, taking in Daniel's appearance for the first time. She stopped mid-step. Despite his best attempts, Daniel's temper had flared, and his fangs had fully descended.

Only a fool would've continued to lecture him at this point. I could only assume it took every ounce of his restraint not to lash out at his former music teacher. If you asked me, she was lucky that her throat was still intact.

Daniel's predatory gaze shifted from Lorraine to Minerva and softened instantly at the sight of his grandmother.

Lorraine turned on her heel and marched away. No doubt she was headed to Mike Mc-Cormick's table to tell him about Daniel.

As soon as she left, I turned to Daniel and said, "I'll be right inside if you need me." Daniel replied with a curt nod toward me before turning his attention back to Minerva. My heart squeezed as I saw the truth register in his grandmother's eyes. I patted her on the shoulder and then made good my promise and turned and walked back inside the gym.

My eyes immediately sought out Lorraine. She didn't disappoint. She was already holding court at her table, spewing hateful words about Daniel to anyone who would listen. I recognized another former student, Christine Epling, standing beside her. The young woman's blue eyes were wide with alarm as she listened to her teacher rant and rave.

"What's that all about?" Clemmie grumbled under her breath.

"Lorraine got into it with Daniel in the hallway."

"Why does that not surprise me?" Clemmie replied.

"Well, it does me. Weren't those two close?" Aunt Thelma frowned.

I thought back to how our former teacher used to fuss over Daniel. He could do no wrong. The praises she used to throw his way were night and day from how she was now treating him. I'd even bet that if you'd asked her two hours ago what she thought about Daniel McEwen, she would've told you he hung the moon in the sky. He was her one student that had made it big, and from the way she talked, she tended to believe it was due to all her hard work. It was those extra voice and guitar lessons that did the trick. I had a feeling Christine was thinking the same thing. From what I understood, the young woman had been another favorite student of Lorraine's. Clemmie had said Christine played like an angel. Although Christine hadn't made it big as far as I knew, but she was still young. Maybe her time had yet to come.

The whole scene was giving me a headache

and making my heart hurt. I stared off, lost in thought, and found myself eying the concession stand over in the far corner of the gym. I spotted Mr. Powell, the band director, standing off behind the counter, his arms folded in a disapproving stance. He, too, looked troubled. He caught my eye and returned it with a head nod. I waved in response and then turned back to Aunt Thelma and Clemmie.

I decided what I needed was a bit of a pick me up, and I knew someone else who could use a break. "I'm going to drop in and say hi to Vance, and then I'll be back, say, in an hour to pick you up?" Clemmie gave Aunt Thelma a ride earlier in the day, but there was no sense in having her drive back around the lake when I was already out and about.

"Better make it a bit longer. It's going to take all of that plus some to replace our inventory."

I looked around for Mr. Whiskers, but I couldn't find the black and white cat anywhere. "Are you sure the rest of your inventory is safe here?"

"It better be. I told Mrs. Potts to take her trou-blemaking cat home. He had no business being here in the first place. No offense," Clemmie said to me.

"None taken," I replied with a smile. I may be

able to shift into a cat with a mere incantation, but even I know there's a time and a place where us four-legged felines are unwelcome.

I left shortly after that and ignored the whispers behind my back as I weaved my way out of the gym. I wouldn't have blamed Daniel one bit if he hightailed it out of town on his own accord. I wouldn't want to stay here with the way people were acting.

Speaking of the vampire, I spotted him in the foyer talking to Chris Montgomery, a Silverlake local and former bandmate of Daniel's from back in high school.

I waved bye as I walked past them.

"Hey, wait up." Daniel pushed off from the brick wall and strode towards me. He dropped his shoulders, and he kept his eyes on the ground as he approached. Everything about his demeanor seemed off. It was such a departure from his usual confident self.

It caught me by surprise. "Are you okay?" I kept my voice low.

"What? Oh, yeah. It's just." Daniel hesitated. I patiently waited for him to find the right words. "I think I need to give Gran some space. I was going to stay with her, but I don't think it's such a good idea anymore. Do you have any open rooms?"

I quickly thought back to tonight's reservations. The inn wasn't full when I left, but that didn't mean it wouldn't be by the time I got back. People tended to book last-minute rooms on Friday nights. "We should. Let me give Percy a call, though, and double-check." I fished my phone out and quickly dialed the inn, bypassing the number of text messages and Misty's missed calls.

"Funny farm, what can I do for you?" Percy said when lines connected.

"Very funny."

"I knew it was you."

"Of course you did. The question is, would you answer it the same if it had been a customer?"

Percy didn't reply, and we both knew the answer was probably yes. "I skipped the lecture and went ahead and asked Percy if we still had open rooms for tonight.

"That we do. Three rooms left. Want me to save lucky number thirteen for you?"

"That would be perfect. Go ahead and put the reservation under Daniel McEwan. I'll settle up with him tomorrow." I looked at Daniel while relaying the information to Percy. I hung up with Percy and turned to Daniel. "You should be all set."

"Thanks. You're a lifesaver."

"No problem. I'll see you in a little bit."

I left Daniel and Chris to their conversation and continued on my way to the car.

FOUR

As I left the high school, I decided to head back over to Village Square and stop at the bakery, La Luna, and pick up a coffee and a sweet treat for Vance. The bakery was entirely out of the way, but everything in the business district closed at 5 o'clock. That meant there wasn't a decent place to grab a cup of coffee other than the high school concession stand, and no offense to Mr. Powell, but Diane sold espresso.

Diane was hanging evergreen garland on the inside of her front glass window when I walked up to the door. Diane stood on a ladder and secured a section of garland before waving as I entered.

"You ditched the vampire already?" she said,

stepping down from the ladder to move it forward underneath the next hook.

The bakery was empty, which wasn't surprising for a Friday night. But, come tomorrow morning, the place would be packed like it always was. Bakeries and weekends just went hand in hand.

"It wasn't just any vampire. It was Daniel McEwen."

Diane gasped. "Oh no, I hadn't heard that part. When did that happen?"

I shrugged. "I don't know. He didn't say."

"It can't be that long ago. I saw him a week or so ago on WNN. Stormy Evans interviewed him about his new album."

"Really." Vance's comment about the thirst of newly turned vampires replayed in my head. I gulped. Could Daniel control himself?

"What's that look for?" Diane asked.

Her comment snapped me out of it. I looked up at Diane, who was back on the ladder. "Huh?"

"You looked like you'd eaten a cursed chocolate."

I hesitated. "Are you sure Daniel wasn't already changed? You know, during the interview."

"Oh, positive. They baked Christmas cookies during the segment, and Daniel joked that he couldn't stop eating them." Diane gave me a pointed look. Everyone knew vampires couldn't eat food.

I grimaced. "This is bad."

"What's bad? What's going on?" Diane came back down the ladder.

I went on to share Vance's warning with Diane before adding, "And he's staying at the inn tonight. What if he can't control himself?" I dropped my voice to a whisper, "What if he attacks a guest?" The prospect was almost too terrifying to verbalize.

Diane's eyes were wide with concern. "Call him back. Tell him you were wrong. You don't have any more rooms." The words tumbled quickly out of her mouth.

"How am I supposed to do that? I don't even have his number."

Diane thought for a minute. "Okay, your next best bet is to do a protection charm around the inn, or better yet, after Daniel checks in, magically lock him in his room."

"Can I do that?"

"Why not? If he asks, tell him it's for his own protection. You know how witches feel about vampires."

Diane did have a point. One that Daniel couldn't deny.

I let out a shaky breath. "Okay, I could do that." Or if I couldn't, Aunt Thelma could.

Diane seemed lost in her thoughts for a moment. "His poor grandmother," she finally said as she climbed back up the ladder and continued to string the garland.

"Poor Daniel, too." I didn't know the story, but he didn't look too thrilled either.

"Sounds like a sad situation all around then."

I agreed that it did. I watched as Diane finished decorating the front window before she turned and said to me, "Now, what can I get for you? Unless you're just here to spin the village gossip. Not that I'm complaining. It's been a week."

"As tempting as that may be, no, I thought I'd get an espresso for Vance and whatever you have in the case that's good."

"He's been working a ton, hasn't he?"

"He has. What with Boyd retiring and wrapping up cases for the holidays, it's been nuts."

"In that case, I have some of Vance's favorite chocolate coconut bars in the back. They should be cool enough by now to box up."

"Perfect, I'll take a few to go with the coffees." I might not be able to lighten Vance's workload, but I could make his night a bit sweeter and let him know that I cared.

Vance walked down the hallway to unlock the front door. I noticed that he had ditched the dress shoes and was left wearing his black socks. I waited as the metal bolt clicked back, and Vance opened the door.

"This is a nice surprise."

I held up the coffee and pastry bag. "I figured you could use a little pick me up." I handed the goods over. Vance leaned down and kissed me on the cheek as a thank you.

"Come on in," he held the door open for me. I waited for the door to shut and then turned and slid the deadbolt back into place before following Vance down the hall to his office.

"Whoa," I said as I entered. Vance tended to be pretty neat and organized, so the fact that his office had papers everywhere was a bit of a shock. "You weren't kidding."

"I know, it's a disaster, right?"

"How many cases are you working on?"

"Too many. I could get ahead if Sheriff Reynolds quit falsely accusing people left and right."

"What's up with that?" Sheriff Reynolds was known to jump the gun, but even this seemed out of character.

"Crime and Christmas never go well together."

"It's that bad then?" I had briefly read about an increase in petty crime in the paper, but truthfully, I'd been too busy with work to follow up on it.

"Part of it is expected this time of year. People tend to get desperate around the holidays when cash is short."

"But this year's worse," I surmised.

"Unfortunately. A pickpocket has been targeting tourists in Village Square."

I thought back to the feeling of unease as I'd walked through Village square. I'd chalked it up to Daniel's sudden appearance, but maybe it had been something else. I would need to be careful and keep my purse close to me at all times, or better yet, not carry cash around with me in the first place.

"Sheriff Reynolds tried pinning it on the Robertson brothers, but he doesn't have any evidence. For once, I think those two troublemakers are innocent."

"That's refreshing." Terry and Tommy caused plenty of headaches for their parents, who always scrambled to cover up for them. One of these times, they wouldn't be able to.

"It is, except Sheriff Reynolds doesn't want to hear it. The only thing he's got on those kids is they were at the wrong place at the wrong time. There's no video evidence. They didn't even have the stolen property on them."

"I say he's got nothing."

"You and me both. And if all goes as planned, the charges will be dropped by Monday morning." Vance looked at the paperwork on his desk.

"But first, you have to submit your counter-argument."

"Exactly. The DA will agree with me once it's all spelled out and he doesn't have the sheriff harping in his face."

"When is he up for reelection?" I joked.

"Not soon enough."

"Too bad there's never anyone to run against him."

"Trust me, I know. The sad thing is, most people think he does a great job."

"That's because crimes are always solved. And no one crosses the sheriff if they can help it."

"Thanks to you," Vance replied.

"That the crimes are always solved?"

"Hm-mm."

"Er, well, thank you," I thought for a moment. "Did I ever tell you how much I appreciate that you don't try and stop my crazy antics?"

"You haven't, but keep talking."

"Well, I do. Truly. The fact that you always have my back means the world to me."

"That's because you deserve nothing less."

"Now you're really trying to make me blush." I playfully swatted at Vance's arm. He caught my hand and pulled me into his chest for a hug.

"You are special, and I adore you, and I will always support you," Vance said with his chin resting on the top of my head.

I pulled back so I could look up at his face. "Even on days when I drive you crazy?"

"Especially on those days." Vance was quiet for a moment and then said, "I'm really looking forward to dinner tomorrow night."

"I know, me too." The thought of a quiet romantic evening with Vance was exactly what I needed. Just the two of us, a nice meal, and nothing but time together. It sounded perfect right about then.

"Want me to meet you there?" Vance usually picked me up or vice versa, but now that I'd seen his office, I knew he'd be working right up till dinnertime tomorrow night.

"That's a good idea. I'll probably end up getting ready here."

"Okay, I'll see you tomorrow night then."

"In the meantime, please be careful. I know you're not worried about Daniel, but I am."

Vance's comment surprised me. The shock showed on my face. I hadn't told him what Diane had said or that Daniel was staying at the inn tonight. It wasn't a conscious decision, but now that I knew how much stress Vance was under, I didn't want to worry him any more than he was. Because the fact of the matter was, I was very worried.

"He's not the same anymore. I know you want to think of him as the same Daniel from high school, but he's a vampire now. Some would even say humanity dies when a vampire's born."

I opened my mouth to protest, but Vance continued. "I can't tell you how many briefs I've read where a vampire has lashed out and killed someone. The defense could line up dozens of witnesses, all swearing what an upstanding citizen the vampire was before they changed, but the moment their heart's no longer beating?" Vance snapped his fingers. "Bloodlust takes over."

I visibly swallowed. "That can't be true." The words on my lips were a mere whisper.

Vance ignored my comment.

"I'd never say anything to Daniel, and it's horrible what Mrs. Springsdale said, but you still need to be careful. I just got you back. I'd hate to have anything happen to you."

"I will, promise." I was sorry Daniel's life ended the way it did, but I had to agree, I'd be happier once he left town and things returned to normal.

FIVE

I took an indirect route to pick up Aunt Thelma, meandering down the side streets of the neighborhood surrounding the school, checking out Christmas lights along the way. Mrs. Potts had outdone herself with a beautiful red and white candy cane display.

The three-foot-tall plastic candies marched down the side of her driveway with swirling red and white twinkle lights brightening her front spruces. She had even carried the theme to her front door, wrapping the wood with red and white striped paper. Her troublemaker cat, Mr. Whiskers, sat on the back of the sofa, staring out the front window. The light of the living room shone behind him. I shook my head as I drove by.

Mr. Whiskers flicked his tail back and forth as if he could tell that I was judging him.

Clemmie's house looked just as festive as Mrs. Potts. She had decorated her small home to look like a gingerbread house, hanging oversized candies on the bushes with white twinkle lights framing each and every window. Multicolored lights that looked like lollipops danced along the driveway and up the front walkway. Her theme was adorable, and it would've been easy to pull off at the inn, something to think about next year.

For this year, I was just excited to show off the property's renovations. It felt nice to welcome guests into an updated version of the place that held so many fond memories from my childhood. I hadn't tackled the outside landscaping yet, but I gathered plenty of ideas as I drove around the lake.

I was still brainstorming ideas for decorating the inn's exterior when I pulled back into the high school parking lot. It seemed I had driven the rest of the way on autopilot. The gymnasium parking lot wasn't as busy as it had been ninety minutes earlier. However, it was still pretty full, which was why I found myself parking further away than I'd planned to. I got out of the car and jogged over to the sidewalk. Behind me, the swing set creaked as the plastic swings swayed on their hinges. The nighttime temperature continued to fall, and I wouldn't be surprised if there was frost on the grass in the morning. Instinctively, I looked down at the ground. The verdant yard had faded with the passing season and served as a backdrop for all the falling red and gold leaves. I always felt that fall was too short back in Chicago. You'd be lucky to have one or two nice weekends before the season seemingly changed from summer to winter.

I'd forgotten how nice a solid twelve weeks of fall could be. Especially now, as the season shifted into winter. Before I knew it, the year would be over, and honestly, I couldn't wait. It was the first time in a long time I'd ring in the new year with my head and my heart in the same place—both full of love and happiness.

Maybe Vance and I could go away for New Year's Eve?

My mind shifted like the changing seasons, and I found myself daydreaming of a tropical vacation. Someplace warm with soft sandy beaches and fruity drinks. I wondered what Vance would think of the idea. I supposed it would depend on how long we could both sneak away from work.

I was mentally reviewing the calendar when someone ran fast and hard into my shoulder. The force of the hit knocked me back, causing me to stumble. I lost my balance and fell backward, right on the ground. My hands hit first, my wrists catching the impact before my backside smacked the sidewalk.

"Hey!" I rolled over on my side in time to see the blurring figure disappear into the darkness. It was Daniel. No doubt about it. No one else in town could run that fast, not in human form anyway. And it had definitely been a man who'd run into me, not a werewolf or another shifter. I stood to my feet and brushed my palms off on my jeans. Instinctively, I rolled my wrists to check to make sure they were okay. Other than being a little sore and possibly bruised, I felt alright. "What got into him?" I thought as I scanned the darkness and continued to rub my wrist.

I hadn't made it two steps when my blood turned cold.

Lying on the side of the gym where the gravel met the grass was a body.

I didn't even think as I raced forward. Time seemed to slow down, and it took me an immeasurable amount of time to reach the person. The woman was lying face down, but I didn't need to turn her over to see that it was Mrs. Springsdale. I bent low to Lorraine and went to check for a pulse. My fingertips reached out before drawing back in shock. Two puncture marks scored the side of her neck. Bright red blood trailed out and seeped into the ground.

Thirty feet away, the side gym door opened. Aunt Thelma, Clemmie, and Christine stepped out into the evening air. Their purses were on their shoulders, and Christine was carrying a cardboard box full of what looked like leftover crafting supplies. At first, the three ladies didn't see me. They continued to walk forward and talk to one another. But the moment Clemmie spotted me, chaos ensued.

"What in the world?" Clemmie started to hobble forward as quickly as her legs would carry her.

"What is it, dear?" Aunt Thelma turned to her. It took her a moment longer to see me on the ground. Christine locked eyes with me and froze. Her mouth dropped open, and she appeared to be unable to take another step forward.

"What happened?" Clemmie came forward and squatted down, resting her forearms on her thighs. She didn't need to get any closer to realize Lorraine was dead. Clemmie spotted the puncture marks before I could say anything. She sprung back on her feet and stumbled backward quicker than I thought the older lady could manage.

"Oh my, Daniel's gone and killed Lorraine Springsdale." Clemmie looked to me and then

Aunt Thelma. Christine stood ten feet behind, as still as a statue. My eyes scanned the darkness for any sign of Daniel, but I knew he was long gone.

"We should get back inside," Aunt Thelma said, picking up on the perceived danger.

"Daniel took off. He ran into me while he was fleeing." I absentmindedly rubbed my wrist.

"He did? My word, what if he'd attacked you? I can't even think about that." Normally, Aunt Thelma was always the one to reserve judgment, but not today. Even she couldn't deny that Daniel was to blame.

"I'm calling the sheriff." Clemmie began to dig in her oversized purse for her cell phone. I started to agree, but then I looked over at Christine. "Better ask for the paramedics too." I motioned with my head over to the young woman. "I think she's in shock." Christine didn't even blink. She seemed lost in her own world.

"I think I'm in shock too." Clemmie fanned herself with one hand while the other held her phone up to her ear.

At that point, other crafters filed out of the gym, all ready to go home for the evening before the big day tomorrow. One by one, gasps rippled through the crowd.

"I think you all should go back inside," I said,

raising my voice. I had a feeling the sheriff was going to want to interview everyone, or he should.

"Good idea, dear," Aunt Thelma said, eying the crowd.

"You heard the woman. Everyone back inside." Clemmie shooed the crowd forward like a sheepdog herding her flock.

I walked over to Christine and tried to steer her away from the body. I gently placed my hand on her elbow and pulled her forward to turn her back from Lorraine. From behind me, I could hear Clemmie on the phone. "Yes, that's what I'm telling you. It's Lorraine Springsdale. She's lying dead right outside the gym door. How? Well, you're not going to believe this, but a vampire bite."

Aunt Thelma fidgeted with the gold chain around her neck as we eavesdropped on Clemmie's conversation.

"I know. I agree. It has to be Daniel. Angelica said he ran right into her as he was running away from the body."

I shot Clemmie a look. I don't know why I felt the need to protect Daniel, but I did. Maybe I was being naïve or just in denial, but I hated thinking Daniel killed Mrs. Springsdale. But even I had to admit he was the most likely suspect. Daniel had the means. He was at the scene. And he had plenty of motivation following their argument. Could Vance have been right, and the Daniel that I had known all those years ago was gone forever, replaced by a bloodthirsty monster? I couldn't believe it. I felt sick to my stomach, and I suddenly realized why Christine looked the way she did, pale as a ghost.

My eyes fell on Christine. "Are you okay? Scratch that, don't answer that. I can see that you're not. Let me see if I can get you something to drink." I was going to ask Aunt Thelma to keep an eye on Christine so I could grab her something from the concession stand, but Mr. Powell popped his head out the door right then and there.

"You need me for anything?"

"Water, maybe?"

"You got it. I'm getting everyone lined up inside here. Make it easier when Sheriff Reynolds arrives." Leave it to the Mr. Powell to handle everything with precision. Law and order were what we needed. Let's hope the sheriff could, for once, deliver it.

SIX

Boy did the sheriff deliver it, and not in the way I'd hoped. With lights blazing on top of his SUV, Silverlake's very own Sheriff Reynolds pulled in the parking lot as if the building were on fire. Two squad cars trailed in after him. The six-foot-tall man hopped out of the truck and strolled directly over to where Mrs. Springsdale lay on the ground. He took one look at the puncture marks on her neck and turned to me and said, "Where's Daniel?"

I hesitated.

"Well?" The sheriff looked to me, Clemmie, and then Aunt Thelma. Mr. Powell had led Christine inside to sit down.

Finally, I found my voice and said, "I'm not

sure. He ran that way." I pointed to the tree line that surrounded the perimeter of the school.

"After he crashed into her," Clemmie added.

"He knocked you down?"

"He did. I don't think he meant to, though."

"You trying to defend him now?"

"I didn't say that." But was I? Honestly, I think I was trying to give Daniel the benefit of the doubt more than anything. I said as much to the sheriff.

He barked out a laugh. "And here I was starting to think you got smart."

"Told you she didn't," Deputy Amber Reynolds said from behind her daddy's shoulder. The sheriff acknowledged his daughter's presence with a head nod. Amber's partner Deputy Jones was the only one who seemed to get to work, sectioning off the crime scene and consulting the medical examiner, Dr. Fitz. I wondered if the werewolf doctor could smell anything off Lorraine's body like I had seen him do in previous cases. However, if he did pick up on anything, he didn't make any indication—no scrunched-up nose or sniffing the air like before. I wasn't sure if that was a good thing or not. I knew the werewolf could smell poison and other shifters, but I wasn't sure if vampires had a scent. I watched with open curiosity as Dr. Fitz continued to work. He took Mrs. Springsdale's temperature and made a couple of notes and remarks to Deputy Jones. The deputy nodded and left the medical examiner's side to approach our group.

"Ladies," Deputy Jones said as he joined us. I replied with a soft smile. Clemmie and Aunt Thelma said their hello's.

Deputy Jones turned his attention to the sheriff. "Dr. Fitz says that she just passed, probably within the last thirty minutes."

I gulped. It hadn't been quite thirty minutes since I'd found Lorraine.

"What time did you find the body?" Sheriff Reynolds turned to me. I looked at Clemmie to confirm the time. She looked down at her watch while Aunt Thelma looked at her phone.

"About twenty-five minutes ago," Clemmie said.

"The same time you saw Daniel run away from the body," Sheriff Reynolds smirked.

"That's right," I confirmed, even though the sheriff hadn't been waiting for a reply.

Sheriff Reynolds turned away from me. "Get an APB out on Daniels. I want every resource looking for him. Tell the town council to seal off the borders. No magical creature is entering or exiting Silverlake without going through me."

I opened my mouth to protest. Surely our

tourists wouldn't want to be held captive in Silverlake.

"It's just for tonight. With any luck, we'll have Daniel captured before sunrise," Sheriff Reynolds continued.

I didn't bother arguing. I knew the sheriff wouldn't change his mind, and hopefully, there weren't any guests planning to leave within the next ten hours.

Amber hopped at her father's commands. The sheriff then turned his attention to Deputy Jones, who seemed like he wanted to say something. "Yes?" the sheriff asked.

"I was wondering if you wanted me to take statements from inside. It sounds like we got quite a few potential witnesses," Deputy Jones said.

"Get names and numbers. Tell folks we'll set up interviews unless someone has something they need to tell us tonight. But as far as I'm concerned, Mr. McEwen is our man."

"What is going on? You found another dead body!" Mayor Parrish's voice shrilled, one notch below deafening, from behind me.

I flinched. I hadn't even seen the woman approach.

"Don't go talking to Angelica that way. It's not her fault Daniel ripped out Lorraine's throat."

I grimaced at Clemmie's remarks.

"Now, we don't know that it's Daniel, dear." Aunt Thelma said, acting more like herself.

"Thank you." I was glad somebody had finally said it, and I was surprised it had taken Aunt Thelma as long as it had.

"But we're pretty sure it's him," she added.

I gritted my teeth. "He's a suspect," I clarified for Mayor Parrish.

"And the only vampire in town, so my money's on him. Plus, he plowed down Angelica trying to run away," Clemmie said.

"Well, find him then! We have a contest to win. This is Silverlake's year. I can't have a murder on my hands. WNN won't come to the crime capital of the paranormal world! Not to mention all those poor witches looking to have their Christmas wishes come true! You have got to solve this case, pronto." Mayor Parrish pointed her finger in my face.

I took a step back and cleared my throat. "The sheriff's right over there if you want to share your concerns with him." Sheriff Reynolds was conversing with Dr. Fitz on the side. The sheriff's arms were crossed comfortably at his chest, and his stance was wide as if he were having a casual conversation. Dr. Fitz made a remark I couldn't hear, and Sheriff Reynolds laughed.

"Oh hosh posh, I like Sheriff Reynolds enough,

but anyone in this town knows if they want to solve a mystery, you're their witch. Besides, Daniel's your friend. It should be easy for you to find him, and don't deny it. I have it on good authority you were with him tonight."

The mayor was doing a fine job of rendering me speechless. I chose my words carefully. "I did run into him tonight and offered to bring him over to the high school." Mayor Parrish shot me a horrified look as if I was somehow responsible for Loraine's murder. "He was looking for his grandmother, Minerva," I quickly clarified. "Trust me, I had no idea what was going to happen."

"Well, whatever brought you two together tonight, and him here, doesn't matter. What matters now is finding him. See to it, will you?" Mayor Parrish was clearly dismissing us, and I wasn't sure what to say.

It turned out I didn't have to say anything. Clemmie spoke for both of us. "You can bet we will," she said with more enthusiasm than I could possibly feel. I looked to my aunt to say something, but she seemed lost in her thoughts. Her thin lips were pursed, and her hand still fidgeted with her gold necklace. Shock or not, it looked like I had another case to solve.

SEVEN

It was close to eleven o'clock by the time Aunt
Thelma and I pulled out of the high school
parking lot. My aunt hadn't said much
during the police interview. Instead, she pulled
out her jewelry-making equipment and continued
to work off on the side. Clemmie, on the other
hand, was talking to everyone and anyone about
Daniel and what had happened. One could say
that the woman had been born with the gift of gab.

"I just can't believe it. Can you believe it? I
mean, I guess I can believe it because he's a vampire and all, but Daniel? He was such a talented
musician." Clemmie went on and on. All that was
missing was her teapot and some scones, and it
would be like sitting down at her tea shop.

"Penny for your thoughts?" I asked my aunt as I navigated the turn into the inn's parking lot.

Aunt Thelma sighed.

"Now, I really want to know what you're thinking," I added as I pulled into the parking spot and put the car into park.

"I think I'm in shock. It's all so surprising, isn't it? And poor Minerva. I feel like I've been saying that all night long, but she is such a sweet lady. First, she finds out grandson's a vampire, and now this?"

"I know. It's heartbreaking." Yet another phrase that I had said more than once that evening.

"Lorraine was rude and outspoken, but she didn't deserve this."

I agreed with my aunt. "Do you think Daniel could be innocent?" I said as I opened the inn's glass door for Aunt Thelma.

Aunt Thelma sighed. "I'd like to think so, but probably not."

I twisted my lips.

Aunt Thelma continued around to the other side of the reception desk and tucked her purse behind it. "Think of it this way. What if it hadn't been Daniel?"

"What do you mean?"

"What if it had been some other vampire. Someone you didn't know, and you saw them run-

ning away from Lorraine's body. Would you second-guess it?"

I didn't even have to think about it. "No, probably not." I felt guilty admitting it, but Aunt
Thelma was right.

"And what if it had been a witch running
away, someone local? Wouldn't you be suspicious
of that person too?"

"You're right. I just feel so conflicted. On the
one hand, I know vampires are deadly, but it's
Daniel. He's a good guy." Or he was. One minute I
was worried about Daniel's safety, and the next, I
was worried about mine. It was mind-boggling.

"As much as it pains me to think that he did
this, it is the most obvious conclusion." Aunt Thelma's words trailed off.

"And yet?" I asked hopefully.

"And yet, you can't go around making assump-
tions, can you?"

"Everyone else seems to think so."

"Which is why it's a good thing you're going to
investigate."

I looked up in surprise at my aunt. Percy, who
had been snoozing behind the counter, woke up
with a start and began to follow our conversation.

"What did I miss?" Percy stretched his arms off
to the side, making the letter Y in the air above his
head as he yawned.

I closed my eyes. "Lorraine was found murdered outside the gymnasium tonight."

"You found another dead body? How come you always get to have all the fun?" Percy asked.

"Only you would think that's fun." I shook my head. "I'm going to go ahead and let Aunt Thelma fill you in on the rest of it. I need to get some rest." My head was filled with too many questions, and my heart was downright troubled. What I needed at that moment was a hot shower and my comfy bed so I could fall asleep fast and think straight come the morning.

I decided to take a nice hot shower, hoping the heat would help soothe my thoughts and ease me into sleep.

Aunt Thelma stayed downstairs, chatting with Percy as I let myself into our third-floor apartment, letting the door click shut behind me. I kicked off my shoes and dropped the car keys in the gold-plated dish by the front door. Since Aunt Thelma and I shared her car, we tried to keep the keys in a central location. That had been my idea, as my aunt was prone to losing everything and anything that wasn't attached to her. I had thought about securing a Bluetooth chip to the keys and even her wand for those times either turned up missing, but Aunt Thelma had scoffed at the idea, insisting it wasn't necessary.

I padded in my stockinged feet to the hallway bathroom, planning to turn the shower on and let it warm up while I gathered my nightclothes together in my bedroom. But the moment my hand slipped through the shower curtain and reached for the faucet, cold fingers gripped my wrist. The assault was so shocking that a scream couldn't even rip its way out of my mouth. I pitched backward, trying to get away. My left foot braced against the edge of the tub as I tugged my arm back. The man pulled the shower curtain back.

"Shhhh! It's just me. Don't scream, please. I need to talk to you."

"D-d-daniel?" I stumbled over his name. I could feel my pulse beat rapidly underneath Daniel's fingertips. Daniel's nostrils flared, and I could tell that he could feel the blood pounding in my veins as well. I willed myself to calm down and slowed my breathing. Trying not to look like such easy prey in the eyes of the predator.

Daniel let go of my wrist. "I'm not going to hurt you. I was only hiding in the shower because I wasn't sure if it was you or your aunt who'd come home." I shuffled backward until the back of my thighs hit the bathroom countertop. Daniel stayed in the shower, keeping his distance.

"What are you doing here?" I inched my way closer to the door, my trembling fingertips trailing along the white countertop, steadying myself. It was a pointless attempt because I was defenseless. It's not as if I could outrun the vampire, and my wand was back in my purse by the door. I could only pray Daniel was telling the truth.

"I didn't know who else I could turn to. I need your help. I didn't kill Lorraine."

I eyed Daniel skeptically.

"I promise you. You have to believe me."

"What, you bit her but didn't kill her?" I tried to make sense of what Daniel was saying.

"No. I didn't do anything. She was like that when I found her."

I couldn't keep the disbelief off my face. With my head cocked to the side, I crossed my arms in front of my chest.

Daniel raked his hand down his face in frustration. "I hate this. No one believes me. No one will listen to me. All because of what I am." Daniel looked up to the ceiling in silent prayer. His gaze fell back down and locked with mine a few seconds later. "Listen, I've never tasted human blood, okay? I can't, or I'll be stuck like this forever."

"What are you talking about? You already are a vampire."

"That's why I'm here. That's why I came home. I'm trying to find a reversal spell. Rumor has it, one exists, and the only way it works is if I never drink any human blood. Not that I don't want to. I'm not proud of how much your blood calls to me, even right now."

I moved an inch further toward the door.

"Everything inside me is screaming for me to drink your blood, but I won't do it. I can't, not if I want to go back to who I was."

I gulped. "Is that possible?" My voice trembled. Given the circumstances, it was a miracle I could speak at all.

Daniel didn't reply.

"I've never heard of it," I said, filling the silence. But then again, I didn't know much about vampirism.

"It has to be. Because if not? I won't go on like this." Daniel didn't need to go into any more detail.

I swallowed nervously. His expression was so pained that it made my heart break. I took a step forward, planning on comforting him. It was Daniel who stepped back.

"You might just want to keep a bit of distance until your pulse comes down," he confessed, looking disgusted with himself.

I jumped back. "Okay, right. How about we get out of the bathroom and come up with a plan."

"You believe me then?"

I might've been signing my death warrant, but yeah, I did believe him. "I do. But first thing's first, I have a phone call to make."

Shockingly, Vance hadn't heard about Lorraine yet. He had been sequestered in his office, and for once, no one had managed to call him before me. I had planned to call him after my shower anyway.

"You're home?" Vance said with sleep thick in his voice.

"Did I wake you?"

Vance cleared his throat. "What time is it?"

"A bit after eleven."

"I must've dozed off, but your home then?" Vance repeated himself.

"I am. But I need your help."

I could hear Vance sit up, the chair creaking on the other line. "What's wrong?"

I filled Vance in on Lorraine's murder and Daniel's involvement, including the fact that he was now sitting at Aunt Thelma's dining room table. "And?" Vance practically growled into the phone.

"I think he's innocent. Truly. I'll explain it all when you get here, I promise."

Vance was silent on the other end of the line.

"Vance?" I said after the silence lingered.

"I'm here," he said on an exhale.

"So, can you come over?"

Vance was once again quiet. I thought now might be a good time to remind Vance that he had just said hours ago how adorable he found me even on days when I drove him crazy, but I held my tongue.

"Give me five minutes." Vance sounded weary. A fresh wave of guilt washed over me, and I hadn't even told him about Daniel's reservation yet.

I replied my thanks and hung up with Vance.

Next, I called down to the front counter, asking Aunt Thelma if she could join me upstairs. This was a situation that called for all witches on deck.

"What's up, man?" Daniel asked Vance as he walked through the front door.

Vance replied with a head nod as he scanned the room as if looking for danger. "How you been?" Vance said, still on edge.

"Can't lie, I've been better."

Aunt Thelma fussed behind us in the kitchen, getting a pot of tea together. I was planning on helping her but thought better of it when Vance arrived. Someone needed to be the middleman and help smooth the reintroduction over.

"I have the tea!" Aunt Thelma's voice trilled from behind us.

"Why don't we all have a seat." I ushered Vance to the dining room table. Aunt Thelma bustled in behind us, a tea tray in hand with place settings for three and a plate of cookies for all. Daniel eyed the tea set longingly. I looked over at my aunt. She blushed, belatedly remembering Daniel couldn't eat.

Aunt Thelma busied herself pouring a cup of tea for myself and Vance. Vance's cup sat untouched as he studied Daniel across the table. I was about to interrupt the staredown when Vance said, "Why don't you tell me what happened tonight?" Vance directed the question to Daniel.

"There's honestly not much to tell. I was hanging out around the school, killing some time when I smelled the blood. It hit me like nothing else. It's hard to explain, but man, I got a whiff of that sweet smell, and my body went into overdrive." Daniel's eyes lit up, and he looked off in the distance as if reminiscing over a fond memory.

I pulled him out of his reverie. "You said you didn't bite Lorraine."

Daniel blinked. "No, I didn't. All I did was

follow the source. As soon as I realized what had happened, I took off."

"Why run?" Vance shrugged his shoulders.

"You have to admit, it does make you look guilty." Aunt Thelma brought her teacup up to her lips and took a sip.

"I panicked. I mean, who wouldn't? I knew what it looked like. Someone set me up."

"To make it look like a vampire killed Lorraine?" Vance wasn't buying it.

"I know it sounds crazy, but what else can it be? I didn't do it. Even if I'd been in my right mind and able to explain myself, who's going to listen?"

"Why weren't you in your right mind?" I asked.

"All that blood? I couldn't think straight. I knew I would drink it if I stayed a second longer." Daniel placed his palms on the table and leaned forward. "I'm trying to be strong, but you don't understand. The feeling, it's intense." Daniel closed his eyes.

"You're telling me you haven't drunk any human blood?" This question came from Vance.

"I can't. If I ever want to go back to the man I was, I have to stay away." I turned to my aunt. "Do you know what he's talking about?"

Aunt Thelma fiddled with her necklace. "I've heard of it, but not for years. I think it might be a potion?" Aunt Thelma looked to Daniel for confirmation, but all he could do was shrug his shoulders.

"I was hoping Gran could help me, and she probably would've if Lorraine hadn't been murdered."

"She still might. I mean, I believe you. And so does Vance, don't you?" I looked to Vance to confirm. I nodded my head in encouragement.

Vance hesitated. "I believe you, but you got to admit, it looks real bad."

"I know, I know. That's why I need your help," Daniel said.

"Okay, let's start over. If this was any other case, what would we do first?" I asked.

"Gather info about the victim," Vance said, seeming to relax for the first time. He rolled up his sleeves and pulled his cell phone out of his pocket, ready to take notes.

"What do we know about Lorraine?" I looked over to my aunt.

"Not much, really. Didn't hang around in the same circles, I'm afraid."

"I haven't seen her much around town, either. I think her work and students keep her pretty busy," Vance agreed.

"There's an angle we can try. We know she

can be pretty tough on her students." I gave Daniel a sympathetic look.

"Even before tonight," Daniel remarked.

"What about personal relationships?" I switched gears. "Is she married?"

"Not anymore. Her daughter and ex-husband still live in town, though," Aunt Thelma replied.

Vance tapped away on his phone. "So, we have possible suspects to be current and former students, and maybe her ex-husband?"

"Probably not Hank. He's had a bit of a rough go over the last two years. He uses a wheelchair now," Aunt Thelma added.

"Okay, so cross ex-husband off the list. But, it's still worth talking to him and his daughter," Vance said. Both Aunt Thelma and I nodded.

"Annabelle's her name," Aunt Thelma added.

Vance wrote that down.

"In the meantime, you need to turn yourself in," Vance directed his attention to Daniel.

"No way. You're out of your mind. They'd stake me first and ask questions later."

I winced.

"There's no chance I'd get a fair trial in this town. I know the way Sheriff Reynolds works."

"He won't give you a fair deal, but I promise you will get a fair trial," Vance replied.

"I agree with Vance. The longer you hide, the guiltier you look."

"Angelica does have a point," my aunt chimed in. "If you turn yourself in on your terms, it can only help your case."

"And it might be the safest place for you. If someone is trying to set you up, which is what it looks like, who knows how desperate they'll get?"

"You think they'll come after him?" Vance looked at me.

"Maybe? I honestly don't know. But they were desperate enough to kill someone the first time."

"And, if we can figure out that spell and turn you back into a witch, that will prove your innocence. Sheriff Reynolds might be a puffed-up buffoon, but even he won't be able to deny that," Aunt Thelma said.

Daniel still looked unsure.

"You have my word. I'll do whatever it takes to set you free. Even if that means breaking you out of a jail cell myself." My voice sounded more confident than I felt, and I only hoped it wouldn't come to that.

EIGHT

It took a bit more convincing, but eventually, Daniel agreed to let Vance accompany him to the sheriff's department.

"Fine, let's get this over with before the sun comes up," he said as he pushed off from the kitchen table in defeat.

"It'll be okay, I promise." Daniel shook his head, not believing me for a second, which only made me want to catch the real killer as soon as possible.

Sleep evaded me that night. I laid in bed tossing and turning, wondering how the questioning was going down at the station and if Vance would call me as soon as he left. Just before seven, I gave up all hope of getting any sleep and got out of bed, deciding to slip downstairs and finish decorating the Christmas tree instead.

The apartment was as quiet as can be as I walked out. I hoped that meant Aunt Thelma was sleeping soundly. My fitful night made me realize how much I should keep one of Connie's relaxation tonics in the cupboard. You could bet I would be stopping by her potion shop sooner rather than later. Not only that, but I wanted to check with Connie about the vampire-reversal spell. Connie was a brilliant witch and potions master. If anyone knew about the magical elixir, it would be her. Unfortunately, Mix It Up! didn't open until ten o'clock on Saturdays, which meant I had hours to kill.

Emily waved at me from behind the front counter. "You're up early," the teenager replied.

"I was going to say the same to you. I thought you came in at eight." Emily was one of the teenagers who worked weekends at the inn.

Emily shrugged. "I'm a morning person. Percy offered me the early bird shift on Saturdays."

"Ah, well, I couldn't sleep. Thought I'd finish decorating the Christmas tree."

"I heard what happened. Do you want to talk about it?"

I looked at Emily. She seemed wise beyond her eighteen years. Still, I wasn't about to talk about the case with her until I remembered that Emily went to the high school where Lorraine worked. "Did you have Mrs. Springsdale as a teacher?"

"Oh gosh, no. I can't read music to save my life. She would've thrown me out!" Emily smacked her hand over her mouth. "I shouldn't talk bad about her, should I?" The young woman looked sheepish.

"No, it's okay. I remember how she could be."

"You had her too?"

I tried not to take offense at Emily's shocked expression. I wasn't that old. Then again, I was twice her age. I remarked that I did have her and then said, "Does she have a favorite student right now?"

Emily pursed her lips while she thought. "I honestly don't know, sorry."

"That's okay. But if you hear anything, will you let me know?"

"Oooh, are you investigating?" Emily's eyes lit up.

I looked around the lobby before replying, "Something like that, which is why I need as many leads as possible."

"I thought that vampire guy killed her?" Emily scratched the top of her head.

"Daniel? No, he's innocent. But that's not what someone wants us to believe."

"Oh, wow. Okay, I'll keep my ears open for sure."

"Thanks, I appreciate it."

I left Emily behind the counter and walked further into the lobby to turn on the fireplace and the radio. In no time, the inn felt nice and cozy, even though my thoughts still ran cold.

Aunt Thelma was still sleeping when I finished decorating the tree. The task hadn't taken nearly as long as I had hoped. Upstairs, I decided to take a shower and get ready for the day. Thankfully, no one gripped my wrist when I attempted to turn on the water this time. You could bet I'd be checking my shower obsessively for the foreseeable future. I even thought about getting rid of the curtain and installing glass doors so no one could hide in my shower ever again.

I looked at the clock after I was put together for the day. Mix It Up! might not be open yet, but Spellbinding Books was. I suppose there was a chance Misty had the reversal spell in one of her books. Either that, or the library, and you know what they say about no stone unturned.

Sneakers laced up and wand at the ready, I headed for the Enchanted Trail, leaving Aunt Thelma her car to drive over to the high school. If

I knew my aunt, she would be up and out of the apartment soon enough. She never took long to get ready. A flick of her wrist and her strawberry blonde hair would be expertly twisted back into an up-do, her emerald eyes sparkling and her complexion glowing. You could say glamour spells were her specialty. That was when she could find her wand.

"Spill it," Misty said, holding her bookshop's doors open for me.

"What, were you spying on me walking up the trail?"

"I knew you'd be here first thing. Now, what happened last night? That was Daniel McEwen you were walking with, right?"

"Yes."

"When did he become a vampire?"

"He didn't say, but it hasn't been long. He's trying to become a witch again."

Misty scrunched her nose. "Is that even possible?"

"That's what I said. But apparently, as long as he hasn't drunk human blood, there's a spell for that. Or maybe it's a potion. Aunt Thelma was iffy on the details."

"And you're trying to find it?"

"It would go a long way to proving Daniel's innocence."

"So, you don't think he did it? I heard Lorraine died of a vampire bite, and you saw Daniel hovering over the body."

"I don't know about the hovering part. But Daniel was definitely there. He plowed into me when he was trying to escape."

Misty's eyes went wide. "And you still think he's innocent?"

"It gets better. Daniel was waiting for me in my shower when I got home last night. Scared the daylights out of me."

"He did not."

I shuddered. "I've already decided I'm installing glass shower doors."

"It does make it harder for someone to jump out at you."

"That's what I'm saying. Anyway, if we can find this spell and turn Daniel back into a witch, then that will prove his innocence."

"And where is he now?"

"Good question. Vance convinced him to turn himself in. They went to the sheriff's department last night. I haven't heard from either one of them since.

Misty shook her head. "Daniel McEwen, man, I had such a crush on him in high school."

I chuckled. "Who didn't? Lead singer, guitar player, those soulful brown eyes?" He portrayed the heartthrob musician to a T.

"And it looks like he only got better with age."

I raise my eyebrows at that.

"From what I could see. It was dark. But were those tattoos on his arms?"

"Yeah, both sleeves."

Misty got a dreamy look in her eyes. "I really hope he's innocent."

I shook my head and smiled. "Why, so you can date him? I thought you were dating Peter?"

Misty waved my question away.

"We were, but we decided to go our separate ways. He's too busy building up his business."

"I could see that. I heard he's opening a store in New York," if Diane had been right, and she probably was seeing she was his mom.

"Yeah, and after that, it's New Orleans, San Francisco, and Austin." Misty bobbed her head side to side as she ticked off each city. "It's fine, really. Peter's a nice guy, but we're at different places in our lives."

"And what, you want to settle down?" I smiled mischievously.

Misty swatted me but smiled all the same. "No, but I am looking at having some fun and hanging out with someone who's not so serious all the time."

I could see that about Peter. He was driven,

and I wasn't surprised he wasn't staying in our small town. You couldn't build the type of company and brand he was trying to build from the back roads of Georgia. Or you could, but you couldn't keep it there forever. Not if you wanted it to be successful.

"Okay, so if you want to help me search for this spell?"

"Let's hit the books." Misty held her arm out to lead the way.

An hour later, with a stack of books on the floor, we weren't any closer to helping Daniel than we were when we'd started. We found spells to help lower your blood sugar, increase platelets, and even change the thickness of a person's blood — all homeopathic type spells to cure medical conditions, but nothing for vampirism.

"Well, that was a waste of time." Misty put her hands on her hips and looked disappointedly down at the books.

"Well, if I ever become diabetic, I know what book I need to read." I held up the thick volume: A Hundred Spells to a Healthier You.

"The spell's probably in some book for the dark arts that I don't carry. They never sell."

"I wonder if we can find it and order it online?"

"You're going to have to look at the table of contents for each book. If not, you'll be buying a whole lot of books hoping that they have something."

"Good point. Let me think about it." I looked at my watch. It was finally after ten. "In the meantime, I'm going to go check in with Connie. Her shop is open, and if it's a potion we're looking for, maybe she might know where to start. Want me to help put these books away?"

"No, it's okay. I got it." Misty looked around her empty bookstore. The morning had started off to a slow start, probably because most locals were headed to the high school, and the tourists liked to sleep then.

I said goodbye to Misty and walked out of the bookstore, making the short trip down the winding path to Mix It Up! I waved at Diane inside the bakery along the way, resisting the urge to pop in for coffee. The same went for Luke at the Candy Cauldron. His Rocky Road fudge was sinfully delightful, and I found myself promising right then and there that as soon as I solved this case, I'd reward myself with a nice thick chunk. Or better yet, I'd get a whole holiday sample platter to share at the inn. How was that for motivation?

Connie's potion shop was a place of wonder. You never knew what she'd be brewing when you walked through the door. Like today, for instance, I had been hoping she was brewing a fresh batch of calming tonic when a putrid smell smacked my face as I walked through the door.

"Oh gross, what is that?" I asked before I could help myself. I clamped my lips shut and held my breath.

Connie frantically poured this and that into the bubbling cauldron behind the counter. "Vampire repellent. Townsfolk have gone nuts demanding it," she hollered over her shoulder as a black mist rose into the air.

"It smells like death."

"That's the idea. It masks the scent of life so vampires can't find you."

"People are that freaked out?"

"My phone started ringing the moment you found Lorraine. I figured I should get started right away before someone tries making the potion on their own. It really is quite tricky. One wrong ingredient and poof!" Connie made a blowing-up motion with her hand.

"I'll let you concentrate on that." I waved the air in front of my face as a fresh round of stink wafted through the air.

"I'm almost done. This needs to simmer for a

good thirty minutes. Oh, in the meantime, here take this." Connie retrieved a small vial filled with rose-tinted liquid from under the counter. "Just pop off the cork and down it. You'll thank me in a minute."

I hesitated briefly, reaching for the potion, but then did as Connie instructed. The moment I swallowed the liquid, the disgusting smell vanished. I looked at the vial in my hand with a new appreciation. "Sometimes, I really love magic."

Connie let out a loud, rich laugh. "Me too, friend. Me too." I handed the empty vial back to Connie and continued to walk around her store.

As promised, Connie sought me out a few moments later. "So, what can I do for you?"

"This might sound crazy, but it has to do with Daniel. He's looking for a spell to turn him back into a witch. Have you ever heard of anything like that?"

"Well, yeah. But it only works if the vampire hasn't tasted human blood, and —"

I cut Connie off. "He swears he hasn't."

"But Lorraine?"

"Again, he says it's not him. He says someone set him up."

"But who would do that, and why? I mean, everyone saw Lorraine verbally attack him last night. You don't do that to a vampire and get to walk away."

"I know, but Daniel swears it wasn't him, which is why this potion is so important. If we can find the spell, and reverse it, then that will prove his innocence."

"Which means there's another killer on the loose."

"Exactly, that's the other part of the problem. I know Sheriff Reynolds is convinced Daniel is his man, but I'm not. Especially after talking with Daniel last night. But I can only focus on one problem at a time, and right now, that's discovering the spell Daniel needs.

"Hang on a minute." Connie motioned with her hand for me to follow her. I followed Connie through the store, weaving around stacked boxes into a narrow hallway. At the back of the store was a small office. Connie ran her finger down the spines of the books on her shelf, stopping when she landed on the one she wanted. She tugged the faded red leather book from the shelf and began to page through. From where I stood, it looked to be a personal journal.

"My grandmother's grimoire," Connie explained. "She was a magnificent witch and wrote everything down."

"That's convenient."

"You have no idea. I had a great uncle once, her brother. Uncle Ernie never turned down a dare." Connie continued to explain while scanning the pages. "Ah, yes, here it is." The potion master slid her finger down the list of ingredients and directions. "It's not as complex as I thought." Connie tapped her finger on her cheek. "I don't suppose he knows who his maker is, does he?" Connie looked up and asked.

"Ah, I don't know. I assume so? Maybe."

"Well, you better hope so because he needs the blood of his sire to complete the spell."

"His sire. As in the vampire who turned him?" I gulped. Hunting down another vampire did not sound like my idea of a good time.

"Afraid so. If you get me that, I can handle the rest."

I let out a shaky breath. "Okay. I guess I'll have to ask Daniel."

"Let me know what you find out."

"Of course. Thanks, I appreciate it."

NINE

When I stepped out of Connie's shop, I checked my phone, and I was surprised to find that Vance hadn't called or texted me yet. I debated calling him but then thought better of it. If he had been up all night with Daniel at the sheriff's department, there was a solid chance he was sleeping right now, and I didn't want to wake him. I trusted Vance would give me a call when he woke up.

But now, I was left with a dilemma. Did I go to the sheriff's department on my own and try to interview Daniel? Vance had referred to me as his associate in front of the sheriff before, but I doubted Sheriff Reynolds would let me talk to Daniel without Vance with me.

My other option was to head over to the high school, check out the craft show, and see what else people remembered from last night. Someone had to have seen something suspicious, whether they realized it or not.

I decided to go with option number two, which meant calling for a ride or taking the trail around the lake.

I was still deciding if I wanted to set off on foot when Diane came walking through Village Square toward me. Her arms were full of bakery boxes. The white rectangular packages were stacked three high, making it so Diane could barely see over the top. I could tell by the twinkle in her eyes that she was smiling when she saw me. Her purse hung from her elbow, and I would bet any amount of money that she was headed out for delivery.

I rushed forward. "Here, let me help you." I slid two of the boxes off from the top.

Diane adjusted the final box and slipped her purse back upon her shoulder. "That's better. Thank you."

"Out for delivery?"

"To the high school of all places. I promised to donate some baked goods to the concession stand. Mayor Parrish can't say I didn't do my part."

I could smell the sugar through the boxes. It made my mouth water. "It smells divine."

"Thank you. I couldn't sleep last night. I might've gone a little overboard with powdered sugar."

"I'm sure you heard about Lorraine then."

"And Daniel. I was going to call you but figured you had your hands full enough. How are you holding up?"

I let out a puff of air. "It's more complicated than you can imagine."

I filled Diane in on the case and the reversal spell on the way across the parking lot to her car."

"You want me to give you a lift over to the high school?"

"You took the request right out of my mouth."

Diane and I got the baked goods settled in the back seat and then climbed into the front, buckling ourselves in.

"You know, it probably makes me an awful person for saying this, but I didn't like Lorraine one bit."

"You didn't? How come?"

Diane navigated out of the parking lot and turned onto the main road that wound around the lake. "It was years ago, and I should probably learn to let go of grudges, but Lorraine's the reason why Peter gave up playing the guitar."

"I didn't know Peter played the guitar."

"Exactly." Diane looked at me and nodded before turning her eyes back to the road. "So he wasn't going to be a rock star or destined for greatness, but Lorraine was so cruel in her criticism of Peter's playing that he gave it up altogether."

"That's awful."

"Especially because up until then, he loved it so much."

"And he never played again?"

"The guitar's still in my basement. Brand-new, mind you. And instruments aren't cheap." Diane shook her head. "I suppose I could have sold it years ago, but part of me always hoped that Peter would want to play again."

"She was something else, wasn't she?"

"That she was."

During the rest of the quick drive, I found myself wondering how many students and parents held similar grudges. The list could be long.

The high school was packed, but this time it was expected. Diane didn't bother looking for a parking spot. Instead, she pulled up to the curb and put her car into park so we could carry the baked goods right in. Inside, the gym was a crush. Shoppers shuffled their feet forward from table to table, unable to move at more than a snail pace given how many people were present. It was loud, too, with people talking over one another. Of course, there was a fair share of laughter and smiles too. After helping Diane drop off her delivery to Mr. Powell, I said goodbye and found my way over to Aunt Thelma's table.

"There you are. Here, set some more of the turquoise earrings out." Aunt Thelma handed me a plastic bag full of more inventory. "I'm glad I stayed up last night making more," she added.

"I'm sorry. I hoped that at least one of us had gotten some sleep."

"What are you two gabbing about over there?" Clemmie asked after handing a shopper their change.

"Beats me," Aunt Thelma said as she picked up her coffee cup on the table and took a sip.

"I'm just saying that I didn't get any sleep, so I was hoping you did," I clarified.

"How come you didn't get any sleep? It's important, you know. I have a tea for that if you'd like." Clemmie looked to her end of the table where she was selling some specialty blends from her shop before waving her hand in the air as a dismissive gesture. "These are all the holiday teas, but you stop in and see me. I'll get you what you need."

"Thanks, maybe I'll do that," I replied even though I didn't intend to. I put the turquoise earrings out as Aunt Thelma had instructed and then stepped back to admire the display.

Aunt Thelma's shoulder bumped into mine. I realized she wanted to have a word with me. I bent my head to the side so that my ear was closer to her mouth.

"What's wrong? You and Vance have a row?" She kept her voice low.

I stood ramrod straight. "What? No. Why would you think that?"

Aunt Thelma threw a hand up in the air, "Because you said you couldn't sleep last night."

"I couldn't sleep last night because of Daniel."

"Daniel? Daniel who?"

Clemmie had now come to stand beside Aunt Thelma. Both ladies were looking at me like I had two heads.

"Daniel McEwen. Remember the vampire who came into town last night and is accused of killing Lorraine Springsdale?"

"Now that you mention it, I think I might've heard something about that." Aunt Thelma looked thoughtful. Now was my turn to look at my aunt and her friend as if they had lost their minds. "You might've heard something about it? What are you talking about? You were there. Aunt Thelma, don't you remember sitting in your kitchen last night talking with Daniel and Vance?"

Clemmie stared down at her friend, waiting for her to answer. But all Aunt Thelma did was rub her temple with her fingertips and shake her head in confusion. "That sounds right, but I honestly can't remember it."

"Well, isn't that something. Somebody's scrambled your marbles," Clemmie put her hands on her hips.

"I think somebody scrambled your marbles too because you were also there," I said to Clemmie.

"In your aunt's kitchen last night?" Clemmie tilted her head back, giving herself a double chin.

"No, here at the high school. You saw Lorraine's body. Don't you remember any of it?"

Clemmie thought for a minute. Her eyebrows creased in frustration. "You're right. I did. But why does it seem all foggy?" Clemmie turned to Aunt Thelma to see what she thought.

"I don't like this. I don't like this one bit." Aunt Thelma shook her head.

"It sounds like you guys know more than you think," I said.

"And someone wants to keep us from remembering," Aunt Thelma added.

The three of us looked around the gym. With so many people, it was impossible to know who had spelled them.

"Hey, I thought I'd find you here." Vance interrupted our trio. He was balancing two cups of coffee in one hand and a donut in the other. He stretched out his hand for me to take a cup.

"Vance? This is a surprise. I thought you were sleeping." I took the cup and blew through the hole in the lid to cool it off before taking a sip.

"No time. Not if we're going to solve this case before the weekend is through."

"That's what we were just talking about." I looked at Aunt Thelma and Clemmie. "Sort of. They don't remember much from last night."

"Someone's messed with our memory, and when I find out who? Ooooh, you bet they're going to get a spell or two thrown their way."

"Which means you know more than you think," Vance said.

"That's what I just said." I then remembered the reason why I wanted to talk to Vance. "How is Daniel doing?"

Vance shrugged his shoulders. I caught him in mid-bite of his donut. I waited for him to finish chewing. "About as good as can be expected. Sheriff Reynolds is convinced he's his man, or make that vampire, but I did persuade the sheriff to let Daniel drink the reversal potion or whatever the spell is when we find it."

"Well, that's great, because I found it."

"You found it?" Aunt Thelma's hands gripped my elbow in surprise.

"I thought you didn't remember much from last night?" I said to her.

Aunt Thelma thought for a second. "Not everything, but bits and pieces are still floating around in there. Wouldn't you agree, Clemmie?"

"I agree, but I still don't know anything about this potion."

That didn't surprise me, as this was the first time I had seen Clemmie since last night. However, now wasn't the time to explain everything. "Only there's a problem," I said to Vance.

"What?" he cocked an eyebrow.

"We need blood from his maker." I pulled the corners of my lips back, making the "eeee" expression. "Connie said the rest of the potion is pretty straightforward. In fact, she was surprised by how simple it was. It's her grandmother's potion," I clarified. "Connie found it in an old grimoire and said she would take care of the rest if we could just get that blood to her."

"Blood spells are nasty," Clemmie said, scrunching up her nose and putting her hands on her hips. "I'm going to leave this one up to you all."

Clemmie seemed to think better of her comment, or maybe it was the three sets of eyes staring her down in disbelief. "Ehrm," she coughed. "Unless, of course, you need me."

"We might need everyone's help," Aunt Thelma replied, looking concerned.

"Okay, but I don't like it, not one bit. Vampires give me the willies," Clemmie shivered.

"None of us like them. Let's just hope that Daniel knows who changed him," Vance said.

"And where to find him," I added. I was starting to second-guess having Daniel turn himself in last night. If he were still on the outside, he could hunt down his maker on his own and hopefully get them to agree to the blood donation. I said as much to Vance. "What's the chance of Sheriff Reynolds letting Daniel go?" Vance chuckled without humor. "Yeah, that's what I figured."

Just then, Christine approached our table with a tray full of chocolates.

"Free sample?" she offered.

"I'd have another, but I've already had three," Clemmie said.

"Oh, one more can't hurt," Aunt Thelma said, plucking a round dark chocolate ball off the tray.

Christine turned the tray to me. "No, I'm good, but thanks. Did you make these?"

"I did, and I have a ton. I may have gotten a bit carried away." Christine nodded toward her table down the row where another lady was working in her place. Every inch of the six-foot table was stacked with her chocolates.

Vance silently took one off the tray, having finished his doughnut. "This place is like heaven," he remarked before biting into the chocolate and exposing a gooey caramel center.

I laughed and shook my head, choosing to stick with the coffee for now, but decided to stop by Christine's table before leaving. I was sure the guests at the inn would appreciate a chocolatey treat, and who could forget how much Percy enjoyed pretending to eat them? Yes, ghosts could be a bit weird every now and then, but who was I to steal Percy's joy?

"I just wanted to say thank you for your help last night," Christine said when Vance was pulled into another conversation, and a fresh set of customers occupied Aunt Thelma and Clemmie.

"Oh, absolutely. How are you holding up?"

"I'm okay." Christine bit her bottom lip, seeming to hesitate before speaking again. "Lorraine wasn't a very nice person, but she was my mentor. I should be sorry she's gone." Christine looked off in the distance. Her eyes focused on something across the way.

"But you're not?" I asked, bringing her attention back to the present.

Christine sighed. "No, I'm not." She smiled a sad sort of smile. "I was grateful for her help, but I could've done without the ridicule."

I thought back to Clemmie's remark about Christine's heavenly talent. "Do you play the guitar as well?"

"Oh no. I mean, I can a little, but what I really play is the violin. Like Mrs. Springsdale does. Er, I mean did."

"Oh. I've always loved stringed instruments."

"Do you play?" Christine's eyes lit up.

"No, unfortunately."

"Well, if you'd like, I could teach you. That's what I do, or one of my jobs anyway. I give lessons." Christine looked so happy. I didn't want to tell her I was a lost cause. I never could read one music note from the next, and I doubted I was any better at it now.

"Yeah, maybe after Christmas."

"Perfect. Let me get you my card. I know it's not what Mrs. Springsdale envisioned after getting me into Havardshire, but I like teaching students." Christine shrugged with the tray of chocolates in her hand.

"You went to Havardshire?" My jaw almost hit the floor. Harvardshire was the most prestigious music academy in the world. Christine blushed. "Now that's impressive."

"Thanks, anyway, let me get you my card."

"Oh, and how about some chocolates too? A couple dozen."

"Okay, great!" Christine walked back to her table.

"What was that all about?" Vance asked me when it was just the two of us again.

"Just trying to brighten a girl's day."

I didn't bother to explain further, and Vance didn't ask.

"What's your next steps?" he asked instead.

"Is that rock candy?" I asked, not answering his question. I motioned to the red crystal candy Vance held in his hand. He brought the stick up to his lips and took a nibble of the hard candy.

"What? It's delicious."

I rolled my eyes. "You better save some room for dinner."

"Come on. I have like six hours until our date." Vance smiled. He knew I was just giving him a hard time.

I shook my head. "To answer your question, I think I'm going to stop by Lorraine's daughter's house next. That is, if Annabelle isn't already here." I looked over at Aunt Thelma. She was selling two pairs of earrings to Mike McCormick.

They were probably a Christmas gift for his wife and daughter. I planned on waiting for her to finish and then asking if she knew where Annabelle lived or if she had seen her already at the craft show that morning.

"While you do that, I'm going to go talk to Daniel. See if I can get a lead on his maker."

"Okay, call me when you find out something, and I'll do the same."

TEN

Aunt Thelma didn't know where Annabelle lived, but thankfully Clemmie did. That was only because Annabelle had moved in to help take care of her father, and Hank lived across the street and two doors down from Clemmie.

"Here, take the car. You need it more than I do." Aunt Thelma rifled through her purse for the car keys. "Oh, blast it. Where did I put those darn things?"

I kept my sarcastic remarks to myself and vowed to order a pack of GPS tags. Aunt Thelma was getting one for Christmas, whether she wanted one or not. "Here, you give it a go. You're better at finding them anyway." Aunt Thelma handed over her purse for me to dig through. I unsnapped the small front pocket, the one where keys were meant to be stored and found Aunt Thelma's car keys immediately.

"Well, now you're showing off." Aunt Thelma tried to act cross, but I could tell that she was secretly glad that I had found them.

I left the gym with my memory thankfully intact and a box full of Christine's chocolates, and drove the short distance to the residential district. I usually try to have a cover when I interview suspects, but today I decided to get right to the point. Something told me that Annabelle would appreciate that.

Mr. Springsdale's home was built like a square. The exterior had been painted a soft light gray, and navy blue shutters framed the windows. A utilitarian cement slab porch led up to the front door.

The house didn't have any decorations except for an evergreen wreath with a big red bow hanging above the detached garage door and a matching one on the front door.

I parked at the street and walked around the car, coming up Mr. Springsdale's driveway. Before I even got to the front porch, a woman I presumed to be Annabelle appeared at the door.

"Can I help you?" Annabelle opened the

screen door and leaned against the doorframe with her shoulder.

I fumbled for the right words. It wasn't that Annabelle's stance was defensive, but it wasn't welcoming either. "Hi, Annabelle?" I stopped walking once I reached the porch, keeping a respectable distance.

Annabelle replied with a nod.

"Hi, I'm Angelica Nightingale. I think you might know my Aunt Thelma?" The woman's expression visibly softened at the mention of my aunt's name. Aunt Thelma tended to do that to people. Everyone in town knew who she was, and almost everyone equally adored her. "I'm sorry for stopping by unannounced, but I'm hoping you can help me."

"I don't know if I can, but I shall surely try." Annabelle held her front door open for me. The door opened into a living room and kitchen combo. The living room was to the right side of the door, with the kitchen to the left. Everything was completely open, except for a small coat closet to my immediate left. An older gentleman, who I assumed to be Hank, sat on the couch watching a show. I wasn't sure what he was watching, but it was a classic, given that it was in black and white. The older man kept chuckling as the scenes played out across the screen, not realizing or caring that he had company.

"Coffee?" Annabelle asked as she led me to the other side of the room.

"Sure, that would be great." I unraveled the scarf around my neck and had a seat at the small four-person table while Annabelle got down two coffee mugs.

It only took a few minutes for me and Annabelle to each have a steaming cup of coffee before us. Between the cup of coffee at the craft show and the one that I was having now, not to mention the coffee I downed this morning while decorating the Christmas tree, it appeared that my day was going to run on caffeine. Some days were just like that.

"So, what can I do for you? You said something about your aunt?"

I took a sip of my coffee to buy some time. "This is really good."

"Thanks, it's a Christmas blend. It has a hint of cinnamon, I think."

I nodded. "I like it." I took another sip and then cleared my throat. "First, I want to say that I'm sorry to hear about your mom." I snapped my mouth shut at the confused look on Annabelle's face. Wait, she did know about her mom, right? It wouldn't be the first time I'd broken the news to a family member.

But then Annabelle visibly swallowed and said, "Thanks, we weren't close, but it's still difficult." Annabelle looked over to where her father was watching TV, lost in his own world.

"He doesn't know," I said, picking up on Annabelle's thoughts.

"No. It would just upset him, and then he'd forget about it tomorrow. It's for the best." Annabelle's voice was filled with sadness.

"I understand." I gave Annabelle a moment alone with her thoughts. Then, when she turned her attention back to me, I continued. "The thing is, your mom got into a fight with Daniel McEwen last night. He's the vampire Sheriff Reynold's has charged with her murder, but the thing is, he swears he's innocent, and I believe him."

"I thought it was an open and shut case?"

"That's what the sheriff wants you to believe, but it's far from being closed. I'm trying to help Daniel clear his name, and I'm wondering if you could help me. Did your mom have any enemies, anyone particular you can think of?"

"If she treated everyone the way she treated me, she had plenty," Annabelle said over the rim of her mug.

"If you don't mind me asking, what happened between the two of you?"

"Oh, it's no secret. I wanted her to help out with Dad. Sure, they were divorced, but she had the means."

"And she said no?"

"She said no." Annabelle tilted her head to the side and left it at that.

Hank's laughter interrupted our conversation. Annabelle smiled while looking at her dad. "He's like a little kid. That part cracks him up every time."

I smiled in response, watching the scene play out.

Annabelle turned back to me. "I wish I could help, but I wasn't close with my mother anymore."

"No, I understand. It was a long shot, but I wanted to check." I took another sip of my coffee. "If you were me, though, who would you talk to next?"

Annabelle thought my question through. "I suppose a co-worker might know a thing or two. Have you already talked to Mr. Powell?"

"Mr. Powell, the math teacher?"

Annabelle nodded. "They're dating."

"Really? I didn't know that. He didn't say any-thing." I thought back to his behavior last night at the crime scene. He didn't even seem upset. I kept the rest of my thoughts to myself.

Annabelle shrugged.

"Thanks, I'll pay him a visit."

The more I thought about it, the more Mr. Powell's behavior last night bothered me. Shouldn't he have shown some type of emotion if he was dating Lorraine? I shook my head in disbelief. I couldn't picture the two of them together. Mr. Powell was a levelheaded, down-to-earth guy, and Lorraine was...I stopped, trying to think of the best word to describe Lorraine. The word caustic came to mind, and I decided that it fit her personality. In any regard, Mr. Powell and Lorraine were opposites.

I didn't need to call Aunt Thelma or anyone else and ask where Mr. Powell lived. He lived just a few houses down from the high school. You couldn't miss his place, where others had put up Christmas decorations, Mr. Powell decorated his yard in Silverlake's blue and silver school colors, complete with twinkling lights and the school flag flying proudly in the front yard.

Mr. Powell answered his front door, and it took me a minute to recognize him. The man's hair was a mess, his shirt was wrinkly, and he held a wad of tissues up to his nose.

"Mr. Powell?" I wasn't sure how I could help the man, but my heart went out to him. I felt terrible for thinking that he hadn't been emotional before. Whatever he was holding back last night, he had let loose since.

Mr. Powell blew his nose into the tissues and then wiped his face, revealing a complexion that was red and swollen from crying.

"Sorry, I'm such a mess." Mr. Powell dropped the tissues on the ground and plucked a few more from the box tucked under his arm and wiped his face some more. In the background, I could hear sports broadcasters calling a game on the television.

"Are you okay? Can I get you anything? I knew Mr. Powell was in his own home, but at that moment, I felt the need to take care of him.

"I'll be all right." But, even as Mr. Powell said those words, a fresh batch of tears streamed down his face. "You want to come in?"

"Sure, thank you." My previous plan of interrogating Mr. Powell went out the window. I switched over to mother hen mode. "Why don't you have a seat. Let me take care of you. Do you have any tea?"

"Thanks." Mr. Powell Sutherland stumbled

over the word. "It's in the cupboard above the microwave."

"Right." I went to work putting on a quick pot of tea while Mr. Powell sat at his kitchen table. "I would've come over earlier, but I didn't realize you and Lorraine were close."

"She was something all right. Not another woman like her." That was one way to word it, I thought in my head. "She had such a fiery spirit, you know? I just loved that about her. I can't believe she's gone." Mr. Powell drew out the last word and choked on a sob.

I eyed the box of tissues that were now on the kitchen table and wondered how many were left, given that piles of tissues littered around the kitchen. "And it's all Daniel McEwen's fault," Mr. Powell said when he composed himself. "If the sheriff hadn't had caught him, I would've hunted him down myself."

"Sheriff Reynolds didn't have to hunt him down, Mr. Powell. Daniel turned himself in on his own. He's not guilty. He's being framed."

"What are you talking about? Everyone knows Daniel's the killer. Listen, I know he's your friend, and I liked the kid and all, but evidence is evidence. It's not like we have a bunch of vampires running around Silverlake." While the tea finished brewing, I went on to tell Mr. Powell Daniel's story.

"So you see, as soon as we make this potion and Daniel drinks it, he'll go back to being a witch. That'll prove he didn't kill Lorraine and that the real killer is still somewhere out there. That's why I'm here. I need your help."

"Daniel didn't kill her?" It took Mr. Powell a minute for the truth to set it.

I shook my head. "He didn't, but someone else did. I'm trying to think of anyone who would want to hurt her."

"Lorraine ruffled a lot of feathers. She was never afraid to speak her mind. But kill her? It doesn't make any sense." Mr. Powell continued to think about it for a few minutes. "I know she didn't get along with her daughter. Something to do with money and taking care of Hank, but I stayed out of it."

"I was just at Annabelle's. She mentioned they weren't close."

"That's an understatement." Hank snorted. "Annabelle was suing her."

"Suing her? Annabelle didn't mention that."

"Like I said, I stayed out of it. All I know is Lorraine made quite a bit of money off of royalties."

"Royalties? What kind?" My mind immediately went to books, but Lorraine wasn't an author as far as I knew.

"Music. Lorraine sold dozens of tunes over the years. She did well for herself. I don't know how well, so don't go asking me, but I know Annabelle wanted some of it."

"Interesting."

"That apple doesn't fall far from the tree," Mr. Powell said, giving me a level stare.

"What do you mean?"

"Annabelle has the same fiery spirit as Lorraine. Those two women together could be explosive."

"You think I need to look harder at Annabelle?"

"I wouldn't take her word for anything."

ELEVEN

I left Mr. Powell after getting him tucked in on the couch with a bowl of soup and a pack of saltine crackers. The teapot was also in reach. Mr. Powell insisted that he couldn't eat a thing, yet the bowl of tomato soup was almost gone before I put my shoes on. I slipped back into the kitchen, grabbed the saucepan containing the rest of the soup, and refilled his bowl before seeing myself out. With any luck and a full belly, Mr. Powell would be able to sleep for a couple of hours. The grief would still be there when he woke, but at least he was still taking care of himself.

Inside my car, I called Vance, but he didn't answer. I shot him a quick text before pulling away from the curb, telling him that I might have a new lead. Perhaps Mr. Powell was right, and I needed to take a closer look at Annabelle. If she was suing her mom, maybe she had gotten tired of waiting for the money and had taken matters into her own hands. I wondered if Lorraine had a will, and if she did, who would inherit her money? And when it came to wills, there was only one man in town to ask.

Aunt Thelma had told me that Boyd was living his retirement years to the fullest. But hearing that and seeing it were two totally different things. Boyd had sold his law firm along with his house and moved into Silver Wand Retirement Community. I had planned to ask the property manager if she knew which condo was Boyd's when I walked into the property's clubhouse and heard Boyd immediately.

"Bingo!" The retired attorney shouted. He held up his hand and waved it in the air. I stopped walking and squinted at the man in the distance. "Boyd?" I mouthed his name. I'd only ever seen the man in business suits, suspenders, and bowties. But there he was, wearing an ugly Christmas sweater and a lopsided Santa hat on top of his head. That wasn't the only resemblance to the jolly old elf. His cheeks were like roses, his nose like a cherry, and Boyd's contagious laughter was just as merry. I couldn't believe it was the same serious attorney I'd interned with all those years ago.

"Can I help you, ma'am?" The dark-haired woman behind the counter stood and leaned forward on the desk.

Her question snapped me out of my shock. "Sorry, I was looking for Boyd. I found him." I pointed to the bingo game in progress.

"Wonderful. Let me know if you need anything."

"I will, thanks." I cautiously walked forward, hoping Boyd wouldn't mind the interruption. An older woman working the game had just left Boyd's side after leaving behind his prize. Boyd and his tablemate, another older gentleman who I didn't recognize, were admiring his winnings.

"I do love me some blackberry jam," the unknown man remarked to Boyd with a hint of wistfulness to his voice.

"On buttered toast." Boyd nodded in agreement, looking just as nostalgic.

I cleared my throat. "Excuse me, Boyd?" I cocked my head to the side and waited for my former employer to recognize me.

"Angelica Nightingale, my word. I'm surprised to see you here." Boyd looked around the room and its lively atmosphere. His countenance changed immediately. "I suppose if you're here, that means you need to talk to me about something important." Boyd kept his voice low and looked at me over the top of his spectacles.

"You would be correct."

"It's a good thing I was finishing up here anyway," Boyd announced. I took a step back so he could scooch his chair back and stand. Boyd knocked on the table with his fist the way someone knocked on a front door. "Roger, I'll see you at dinner."

The previously unknown man waved his goodbye without looking up. Roger was too busy searching his bingo card for the call numbers.

The retirement center was set up with the clubhouse in the middle and glass hallways branching out like spokes on a wheel to the different housing sections. Residents could choose to walk down the glass hallways or go outside and use the sidewalks when the weather was nice. Seeing it was chilly, Boyd decided to stick with the inside path. Sunlight filled the narrow hallway, making the area warm and toasty and causing me to forget that it was December outside.

Boyd waited until we were away from the clubhouse and headed down a private corridor before speaking. "What's it this time?" he asked without preamble.

"A will. And I'm really hoping you can help."

Our conversation was cut short. Another witch, using a walker decked out with green tinsel and battery-operated Christmas lights, approached from the opposite direction. Boyd gave her a polite nod and said, "Hello, Marigold," as she passed by.

"Boyd," the old lady replied with a smile. I smiled at Marigold in turn.

Up ahead, there was a small alcove with a table set for two. A partially completed puzzle took up the round tabletop.

"Will this work?" Boyd offered.

"Yeah, this is great. But are we stealing somebody's spot?"

Boyd seemed confused for a minute until I motioned down to the puzzle. "What? Oh no. They have half-finished puzzles all over this place. They want you to sit down and finish them." By they, I assumed Boyd meant the community staff.

I pulled out the black metal framed chair with the wooden seat and sat down.

Boyd did the same.

"So, what happened now? I'm embarrassed to say I'm not in the loop anymore."

"That's okay. I don't blame you." When I retired, I wasn't planning on following gossip and solving crime either. "I assume that means you haven't heard about Lorraine Springdale."

"Lorraine? What's happened now. Did she get in a fight with her daughter again?"

I grimaced. "It's worse than that." I relayed last night's events, ending with the speculation that Annabelle may have murdered her mother for the money.

"Wowzer, that is a doozy and not a bad theory, either. Annabelle sure had the motivation."

"So, you know about the lawsuit?"

"I do, but as you know, attorney-client privileges supersede death."

I sat back in the chair. "Meaning, you can't tell me about it."

"I can't tell you about the lawsuit, but what I can tell you about is Lorraine's will. My practice didn't draw it up or file it, but Annabelle came around asking about it. In fact, it was the last week I worked. She brought her mother's will to me and asked me to take a look at it."

I leaned forward on the table. My fingers absently played with the pieces of the puzzle before me. "What did she want to know?"

"She wanted to know if there is a way to check if it was current."

"Current?"

"Lorraine changed some documents after the divorce. Annabelle helped her. Pretty standard."

"And was it? The most recent will?" I clarified.

"Beats me. I told Annabelle that I didn't draft it, and she could check with the courthouse if Lorraine ever filed it."

"Did you, by chance, read it?" I asked hopefully.

"No, afraid not."

"But there's a chance Annabelle was the beneficiary, right?"

"I'll tell you the same thing I told Annabelle, check with the courthouse. If Lorraine had changed her will and worried about it being contested, she would've filed it at the courthouse. She should have anyway, and if I were representing her, I would've told her the same thing."

I sighed. "Too bad the courthouse isn't open today." If there ever was a time that I wished it wasn't Saturday, it was today.

"Not to the public, but Shelley's there." Boyd sat back, looking rather pleased with himself.

"Shelley who?"

"Shelley Beaver. She works Tuesday through Saturday. Says she can't get any filing done during the week with all the interruptions. Mayor Parrish agreed to let her work Saturdays in exchange for Mondays off."

"Did she now?" It was great that Shelley was there, but Boyd's comment had me thinking I'd reach out to Mayor Parrish instead. She was the one that had insisted I solve the case, so she should be the one to meet me at the courthouse and help me find Lorraine's will.

"Boyd, you're a genius." I reached across the table and patted the gentleman's hand.

"Well, I don't know about that." Boyd stammered, but with the way his eyes twinkled, I could tell he was pleased to be of service.

"I'm headed over to the courthouse right now."

"If you need anything else, you know where to find me." Boyd pushed back off from the table and stood before checking his watch. "Oh, it's almost time for the poker tournament. I have a title to defend, you know."

"Good luck with that, and thanks again."

Boyd and I parted ways at the clubhouse, and I waved to the dark-haired woman behind the counter on my way out the door. Once again, I checked my phone to see if Vance had called or texted, and I was surprised that he hadn't. It had been a few hours since we had parted ways, and I was hoping to have an update from Daniel by now. As much as I was looking forward to my date with Vance, I would have been willing to put it off to hunt down Daniel's maker. Not that I was looking forward to it, but it was inevitable, and I'd rather get it out of the way and clear our friend's name once and for all than have it hanging over our heads. I could only cross my fingers that Daniel knew who changed him and how we could find him.

TWELVE

"Hell-o!" Mayor Parrish's voice trilled into the phone when our lines connected.

"Hey, Mayor. It's Angelica. I need your help with this case."

"My help?" Mayor Parrish scoffed on the other end of the line.

"Yes. I need a copy of Lorraine's will. Boyd said it was most likely filed at the courthouse. Can you meet me there and help me search for it?"

"Me? You don't need my help. Shelley Beaver works Saturdays. I'm sure she'll be able to give you a hand."

"You know what they say. Many hands make light work." I wasn't sure why I was giving Mayor Parrish such a hard time. Maybe it was because of the way she bossed everyone around lately without doing much of the work herself. It would be a nice change of pace for her to get her hands dirty, so to speak.

"But, I'm at my last dress fitting. You know for the gala on New Year's Eve?"

"The gala that we haven't even won yet?" I replied dryly.

"Yes, but we will. One has to be optimistic about these sorts of things."

"Even if we have an unsolved murder in our town?"

Mayor Parrish faltered, and I knew I had her.

"I'll be right there," she replied succinctly and clicked off the line.

I shot off another text to Vance on the off chance he was done with Daniel and wanted to meet up. I had been speaking the truth when I'd said many hands make light work. The more people we had working on this case, the faster we could solve it.

I was shocked when Mayor Parrish beat me to the courthouse. She stood on the steps bundled up in a brown fur coat with a matching hat fit for an ice princess. I zipped my fleece up and jogged up the steps.

"I hope you're right about this." Mayor Parrish took the gold keys out of her purse and unlocked the front door, making sure to lock it behind us. Mayor Parrish's heels clicked on the marble floor as we walked down the hallway, stopping in the records office. Shelley was jamming to Christmas music and hadn't heard us arrive.

Spell-in' around the Christmas tree

At the witch's party hop

Mistletoe hung where you can see

Every wizard tries to stop

"AHHHHH!" Shelly screamed when Mayor Parrish tapped her on the shoulder. Shelly whirled around and smacked her hand to heart. "You gave me a heart attack.

"Yes, yes, very sorry about that." Mayor Parrish replied in a tone that indicated she was anything but. "We're looking for your help. Where do we file wills?"

Shelley was still trying to catch her breath. "Wills, did you say?"

"Yes, wills. You know, the thing that tells people what to do with your money after you die?" Mayor Parrish replied.

Shelley pushed her dark-rimmed glasses up on her nose. "Is the person living or deceased?"

"Deceased, as of yesterday," I added in case that made a difference.

Shelley's lips made an oh shape. "You're looking for Lorraine's will."

"Have you seen it?" Mayor Parrish asked, looking around at the stacks of papers and boxes Shelley had yet to file.

"No, but it's probably over there in that tall black filing cabinet, or it could be in that brown box, or maybe that one over there, depending on when she dropped it off." My eyes followed Shelley's finger with every box she pointed to. Shelley hesitated. "I suppose it could already be uploaded to the system. I'm trying to move everything to digital, but it is taking longer than I ever imagined."

"Well, which is it?" Mayor Parrish asked in frustration.

"I'm not sure," Shelly confessed. "I can check the computer first. Do you want to check the black filing cabinet, and Angelica, start with that box over there?"

"I suppose. I just don't understand why we have this mess. I thought you filed every Saturday."

"I do, but nobody filed anything for fifty years. It's a lot of work." Shelley looked like she was about to cry.

I stepped in. "It's okay. If the will is here, we'll find it." My comment made me think of something else. "Is there a spell we could use to help us?" I thought of the tracking spells and the summoning charms I'd used before.

"Do you know what it looks like?" Shelley asked.

"Like a regular piece of paper?" I guessed. I didn't think there was anything remarkable about it. But I knew why Shelley was asking. Usually, when you do a summoning charm, you have to imagine the object in your head perfectly. The closer you are to picturing it, the luckier you'd be that this charm would work. As for tracking charms, those required you to love the item, or in my previous experience, the person you were looking for. I didn't think any of us could say that we loved Lorraine's will.

"I'll start over in that box," I said, admitting defeat.

"I found it!" Mayor Parrish shouted from the back of the room two hours later. The petite woman rushed forward, waving the piece of paper above her head like it was a winning lottery ticket. "Here it is!"

Shelley and I rushed forward to meet Mayor Parrish in the middle of the room. Mayor Parrish placed the will on the center counter. Together the three of us peered over the document, reading as we did so.

"I, Lorraine Marie Springs Dale, declare this my last will, yadda, yadda, yadda," Mayor Parrish improvised as she read the will aloud. "Come on, get to the good stuff." Mayor Parrish flipped the page and continued to use her finger to scroll through the text until she landed on the bequeaths.

"Let's see. I hereby leave 100% of my financial holdings to my daughter Annabelle Murray Springsdale."

"I sucked in my breath. Annabelle does inherit everything."

Mayor Parrish continued reading. "Everything except a few minor bequeaths to family and friends. Looks like a couple of musical instruments, a necklace to a niece, and that's about it."

"Annabelle inherits," I remarked to myself more than to anyone. Both Shelley and Mayor Parrish kept a curious eye on me. "But is it enough?" Was money enough motive for murder?

And where was Annabelle last night? I should've asked her earlier today.

I didn't say another word about the case. I wanted to be careful not to jump to conclusions. Sheriff Reynolds did enough of that for both of us. "Can I get a copy of that?"

Shelley nodded and set off to make a copy of the will right away.

"What are you thinking?" Mayor Parrish sidled up close to me.

"It might not be anything. But we need to find out where Annabelle was last night." I kept my voice low. I looked down at my phone. Time had flown by. Annabelle's alibi was going to have to wait. I had a date to get ready for.

THIRTEEN

In a little less than an hour, I was sitting at a table for two at Simmering Spoon, waiting for Vance to arrive. After setting out Christine's chocolates and helping Aunt Thelma set up a hot chocolate bar for the guests, I had let my aunt work her magic on me. Aunt Thelma went all out with a glamour spell. I had told her it was because I didn't have the time to look my best, but in reality, I had wanted to knock Vance's socks off. We might spend the entire evening talking about murder and suspects, but at least I'd look good in the process.

Instrumental Christmas music played over the restaurant's speakers. The tune was soft and occasionally drowned out by the ebb and flow of conversation around me. I sipped my glass of merlot and tried to sit back and relax, but instead, I found myself fidgeting with the cloth napkin on the table. I had already inspected and rearranged the silverware twice. I'm not going to even admit to how many times I checked my phone. I stared at the flame of the oil candle before me. The small candle sat on a square mirror, reflecting the warm glow from the flame. It wasn't like Vance to be late, but I was willing to give him a pass, given how much stress he had been under.

However, as the clock struck closer to half past the hour, I grew worried. My phone calls and text messages to Vance had gone unanswered. Earlier, I thought he needed space to work, but now I was second-guessing myself.

I tried Vance's phone one more time, both his cell phone and office line, but he didn't pick up either.

I signaled for my waiter after Vance's voicemail picked up yet again. A young man, who looked about as comfortable wearing a bow tie as Vance would, stopped by the table. The kid fidgeted with the cloth tied around his neck, using his index finger to pull it away from his throat.

"Hi, I was supposed to meet someone here, but he hasn't shown. I'd like to pay for the wine and leave a note with the hostess in case he shows."

"Okay," the kid said, and really, what else was he supposed to say? I went to fetch a twenty-dollar bill out of my wallet when I realized my wallet was empty. "That's odd." I looked over at the waiter.

He stared at me like he had no idea what I was talking about.

"I'm missing money," I went on to explain. The young waiter immediately appeared uncomfortable. He shifted his weight from foot to foot and eyed someone across the room, most likely the manager.

"It's okay. I still have my credit card. I'm just wondering what happened with my money." I retrieved the plastic charge card out of my wallet, thankfully that was still there, and handed it to the kid.

While the waiter rang up the wine, I tried to think of where my money would've gone. The cash had been in my wallet last night when I'd stopped by the bakery. There were two twenties and a ten-dollar bill. I hadn't bought anything since.

I then remembered Vance's comment about a pickpocket working Village Square. Could they have targeted me without me knowing it? I couldn't see how or when, but maybe that's what made the thief so successful. Then again, I might be getting ahead of myself, and I'd find the fifty dollars someplace random, like at the bottom of my purse. As I said those words, I proceeded to dig through my bag in hopes of finding the missing bills. I was still searching when the waiter came back with my receipt and a pad of paper.

"For your note," he said tentatively.

"Oh right, thank you." I signed the credit card receipt and then used the same pen to write a note for Vance, asking him to call me if he stopped in. Then, standing to leave, I walked the message over to the hostess stand. "Do you know Vance Blackwell by chance?"

The hostess started to shake her head no, but then the manager joined her. Sid knew me and Vance both from our frequent dining.

"Angelica, is everything alright tonight?" The attentive manager asked. He was dressed smart in a cranberry-colored button-down shirt and coordinating black vest, and dress pants.

"I'm not sure. I was supposed to meet Vance, but he hasn't shown. We'll have to take a rain check on dinner tonight."

"I'm sorry to hear that." Sid seemed genuine in his concern.

"Me too. Listen, if Vance stops in, can you tell him to call me? I'm headed to his place now."

"Absolutely. If there's anything I can do to help, let me know."

"Thank you, I appreciate it."

I did just as I told Sid I was going to and drove directly to Vance's. I tried to keep my emotions in check as I headed to the other side of the lake to Vance's apartment. There had to be a logical explanation for where he was, and not someplace horrifying like lying dead on Enchanted Trail. I shivered and shook the image away.

No, Vance had to be okay.

Maybe he had lost track of time and was still at work, or perhaps he was negotiating for Daniel's release, as improbable as that was.

Another thought, and one less pleasant, forced its way in my head. What if Vance had a lead on Daniel's maker, and he had set off to find him on his own? As the thought crossed my mind, it took hold. A feeling of dread settled in my stomach. That was just the sort of stupid brave thing Vance would do.

My heart felt funny as it beat in my chest, and my head felt dizzy. The world seemed to slip on its axis, dropping a few degrees and leaving me off balance.

I realized I was having a panic attack, and it wasn't only because Vance might be facing a vampire on his own. That was horrifying enough. But what would I do if Vance was turned into a vampire too? It would be up to me to save both Vance and Daniel, and I was scared I wouldn't be smart or strong enough to do it. I hated that any of us were even in this position.

The what-ifs had free reign over my thoughts. It was a slippery slope, and I didn't know how to stop myself from sliding into the gutter. But, just as I felt the despair close in all around me, the tiger's eye around my neck grew warm, acting as a talisman, reminding me of who I was and the strength I possessed.

I had to stop my imagination from running wild. Instead, I focused hard on bringing myself to the present.

Somewhere, lost in my thoughts, I had pulled over on the side of the road. My eyes focused on the setting sun. That was real. I felt the leather stitching of the steering wheel beneath my fingertips. That was real too. I rolled down the window just enough to let a stream of cold air filter through. I lifted my fingertips from the steering wheel and held them up to the crack. The cold was real. As was the softness of my sweater and the warmth of the tiger's eye around my neck.

Don't freak out until you have a reason to. I rationalized with myself as I eased off the shoulder and back onto the road.

I can't explain the relief that flooded through me when I spotted Vance's truck parked in front of his apartment. I tried not knocking like a banshee on his front door but failed miserably.

"Angie?" Vance said, scratching his tousled hair. He squinted at me from the other side of the door before using his fingertips to rub the sleep from his eyes.

"You were sleeping?" A mixture of emotions raced through my body. Relief that Vance was okay. Confusion that he had been asleep. Hurt that he'd forgotten our date. It was all too much.

Vance didn't catch any of it. "Yeah, what time is it?" He yawned and stepped back for me to come in.

"Almost seven. You didn't show for our date." I guess hurt was the emotion that won out in the end. I followed Vance into the living room. The television was on low, some Hollywood blockbuster, and Vance had made the couch up for an afternoon nap with a pile of pillows and an oversized blanket.

"What date?" Vance sat down and reached for the remote, clicking the television off.

"Remember, dinner tonight at Simmering

Spoon? You made reservations. We were both looking forward to it." Not to mention I let Aunt Thelma glamour me all up. Speaking of simmering, my temper was doing a fine job of bubbling below the surface.

I stood behind the couch with my arms folded across my chest.

Vance's eyes clouded with concern. "I feel like I should know what you're talking about, but I don't." Vance grew silent until he said, "What day is it again?"

I closed my eyes, instantly realizing what had happened. My anger deflated as quickly as my ego. "Oh, no. They got you too." I didn't want to open my eyelids. The day suddenly felt very long. Too long. I braced myself on the back of Vance's couch. My fingertips gripped the leather for support.

"Who got me? What are you talking about?"

Reluctantly, I opened my eyes. All traces of sleep on Vance's face were gone. He sprung to his feet as if ready to charge into battle. The only problem was, neither one of us knew who we were fighting.

"What's the last thing you remember?" I asked hesitantly.

Vance began to pace. "I saw you this morning at the high school, right?" I nodded my head in confirmation. "You were going to go somewhere. It had to do with..." Vance's forehead wrinkled in concentration. "What did it have to do with again?" Vance looked at me.

"I went to interview Lorraine's daughter, Annabelle. Do you remember anything about Lorraine's death and Daniel being a vampire?"

"Yes?" Vance hesitated, and I wasn't sure how much he remembered at all.

"Sheriff Reynold's charged Daniel in Lorraine's murder. Only we know he's innocent. You were supposed to talk to Daniel and find out who his maker is and see if we can get him to donate some blood." That was about as succinct as I could be. "I'm assuming you didn't do any of that."

"No, not that I know of. I think I came right here and fell asleep because one minute I was talking to you in the gym, and the next you are knocking on my door."

"And there are about six hours in between there."

"That can't be right." Vance rubbed his forehead as if he couldn't believe it.

"It's the same thing that happened to Clemmie and Aunt Thelma. It's like someone put a fog over you."

Vance exhaled. "You're right. Course you're right. And, listen, I'm sorry this happened. Now that I think about it, I remember our date. It's in here somewhere" Vance looked up, and I knew he meant that our date was somewhere in the back of his mind. "I don't know how I could've forgotten it, and you look," Vance took a good look at me for the first time that night. "You look amazing. I'm sorry I ruined tonight."

My temper flared again, and this time the energy wasn't directed at Vance. "You didn't ruin anything. It's whoever's messing with everyone's memory that's to blame, and we need to figure out who that is, fast, before they have a chance to mess with anyone else."

"Or kill again."

"Yeah, that too."

FOURTEEN

Vance was still a bit out of it. The adrenaline rush he'd felt at being spelled, and mine over worrying about him had left us both exhausted. I didn't feel right leaving him alone, which was why when Vance suggested we order takeout and watch a movie, I readily agreed. Neither one of us was up for solving the case that night. The day had caught up with me, and what I needed more than anything was rest.

I woke up the next morning curled up on Vance's couch. He was snoozing peacefully in the recliner. We must've dozed off sometime in the middle of the night.

I was wrapped up warm and snuggly in the blanket with my head propped up on a pillow. My body sunken into Vance's brown leather couch. For a moment there, I was worried I might've been spelled too considering how soundly I'd slept. I was content to lie there as I mentally recalled the previous thirty-six hours.

No, my memory was still intact. Thankfully I had texted Aunt Thelma last night after tracking down Vance to let her know where I was. I hadn't intended on spending the night, but I knew Aunt Thelma wouldn't have stayed up worrying about me. That was all that mattered.

Vance was snoring softly from his corner of the room, and I didn't have the heart or the need to wake him. Instead, I scribbled a note to call me when he awoke, and I let myself out.

The wind that had plagued Silverlake most of the weekend had let up. The air still had a nip to it, but it wasn't as cold.

I popped back briefly in the inn and got freshened up for the day before turning around and heading right back out, waving to Emily behind the front counter as I did. My mind hadn't been firing on all cylinders last night, and this morning I wanted to have some time to think the case through.

One of my first questions was who was messing with people's memory, and how were they doing it? Because I was pretty sure that same person was the one who had killed Lorraine, or they were trying to protect the person who did. The obvious explanation was a spell, but I thought someone would notice a witch raising their wand and hexing people left and right. My second theory was one that I had seen before but was more complex. A witch could create a fog to blanket the gym and affect people's memory in mass, but my memory would've been impacted too if that were the case.

These thoughts whirled through my head as I drove over the Village Square. I planned to grab a cup of coffee from Diane and maybe run my theories by her if she had a moment or two. As I walked down the cobblestone path toward the bakery, I spotted someone up ahead who I knew. Make that three people I knew — Sally, Luke's sister from the Candy Cauldron, and her twin daughters. The tweens were window shopping, and from the sounds of it, they wanted everything that they saw.

"How about a new cloak? A velvet one. I always wanted a velvet one. It would make me look very distinguished," Beatrice insisted.

Sabrina snorted. "You, distinguished?"

"I am distinguished."

"And pigs fly." Sabrina giggled.

"You take that back!" Beatrice demanded.

"I will not!"

"Sabrina, I'm warning you."

"Girls, no one is going to get anything if you keep it up." Sally's voice held enough edge to it for her daughters to realize she meant business. The fact that it was almost Christmas couldn't hurt either.

"Hi Sally, how's it going?" I said as I approached.

"Angelica, good to see you." Sally kept a watchful eye on her daughters.

The peace between Beatrice and Sabrina hadn't lasted long, and the girls were already back to arguing. "You would think they could get along for five minutes." The girls had taken to chasing one another around the holiday decorations, weaving in and out of winter gardens, and kicking up wood chips along the way. Sally opened her mouth to holler at the girls once more but then thought better of it. "I might save my breath. Just this one time."

It was just as well. The girls came to a screeching halt in front of the jewelry shop. Their heads were bent low together as they admired a piece through the glass storefront. Katie, who now owned the jewelry shop after Lyle Peters' death, was a talented designer. I could only imagine what the piece looked like. Sally sighed with contentment as she watched the scene. "You might not believe this, but I'm going to miss having my weekends off."

"I thought you worked for Constantine now?" Constantine was our town healer, a witch who incorporated more spells and potions into her practice than traditional medicine, and Sally was a nurse. "Has the practice picked up weekend hours?"

"No, I still work for Constantine. Part-time, though." I was about to ask Sally if she had decided to go back to the hospital. I know she hated working long hours, but Luke had hinted about Sally needing the extra money from time to time. It couldn't be easy being a single mom. But, before I could ask, Sally explained, "I took a job working for Mr. Springsdale. I'm not sure if you know him."

Sally's remark caught me off guard. "Annabelle?"

"So, you do know him. Annabelle hired me to be her dad's nurse, or I should say re-hired. After leaving the hospital, I worked for her for a while, but she had to let me go. I didn't ask, but it sounded like money was tight."

"And now?"

"Now she's given me a big raise, and with the holidays around the corner? I couldn't refuse."

I wasn't sure how to say what I wanted to

know, so I just came right out and asked it. "Did Annabelle say where she got the money?"

Sally was watching her daughters again but then turned toward me. Her expression seemed sheepish. "I assume she inherited it. I didn't ask."

"I guess I wouldn't have either."

"Girls, get back here!" Beatrice and Sabrina had disappeared around the corner up ahead. "Sorry, I better run. It was nice seeing you!"

Before I could even respond, Sally ran after her daughters.

I watched Sally chase after the girls. No sooner had she disappeared around the corner did Christine come around the other side with her hands full. Literally. She was holding four leashes, and one of the dogs, an energetic lab, seemed to be walking her.

"Bentley, slow down!" Christine tugged back on the leash to try to slow the lab down. "Lily can't keep up!" Christine looked down at the white terrier whose legs were working double-time to keep up with the energetic pup's pace. Bentley ignored her, despite Christine's commands. I picked up my pace to meet Christine halfway and take the smaller dog's leash from her hands.

"Thank you. My goodness, this boy is a brute."

"But he's so handsome," I said, scratching Bentley behind his ears. Not wanting to be left out, Lily jumped up on her hind legs. Her front paws scratched at my jeans. "You're a good girl, too," I said, switching the attention over to Lily. Bentley pranced in front of me, begging for me to pay attention to him once more.

"You do have your hands full, don't you?" I said, looking up to Christine.

"Thankfully, it's only for a half-hour. These are Vicki Love's dogs." I knew who Vicki was. She worked for Misty at the bookstore. "She twisted her knee hanging up outdoor Christmas lights, and it's still pretty tender."

"Oh no, I hadn't heard."

"Constantine's been by a couple of times, but as soon as the pain-relieving potion wears off, Vicki's back off her feet."

"And you're walking the dogs."

"I know, I wish I could do more than twice a day, but with the craft show and my lessons, it's all I can fit in. Bentley isn't too happy."

"I can see that." Bentley had taken the hanging leash in his mouth and was now shaking his head violently, trying to get Christine and me to wrap up our conversation. "Vicki offered to pay me double, and I wish I could take her up on it, but I just don't have the time."

"Maybe I can stop by and help. Tell Vicki I'll give her a call."

"That would be great. I'll let her know." Bentley gave a forceful tug on his leash that sent Christine stumbling forward and almost caused her to fall. "Okay, come on, guys. Let's go." Christine reached out and took Lilly's leash from me before scooping the small terrier up and tucking her partially under her arm. "You ride up here with me. It'll be safer that way."

I waved goodbye and was backtracking toward the bakery when my cell phone rang. It was Vance.

"Good morning," Vance said. "Did you sleep okay?"

"Yeah, surprisingly."

"I know, I feel the same way. So, what's your game plan?"

"I'm going to stop by Diane's for a cup of coffee. Something Sally just said has me thinking. Do you want to meet me at the bakery?"

"Sounds good. I'll see you in a few minutes?"

"I'll be there."

It was foolish of me to think that Diane would have a minute to spare, given the fact that it was Sunday morning. A line, five people deep, greeted me when I walked in the door. Most of the tables were full, too. Locals and tourists alike were indulging in flaky croissants, cream-cheese topped danishes, and heavenly chocolate eclairs. I had planned on only going for the coffee, but now I wasn't so sure.

Ten minutes later, I had a pastry bag full of goodies and two large cups of coffee. I slid into one of the last open tables as Vance walked through the front door.

I waited for him to join me.

"Perfect timing."

Vance tugged off his leather gloves and took a seat opposite of me.

"I wasn't sure what to get, so I got a little bit of everything."

"Nice." Vance peered into the pastry bag and selected a glazed donut. "Two days in a row. How lucky can I get?"

"What did you say?" Seeing Vance with the donut made a lightbulb in my head go off.

"What? Why are you looking at me like that?"

The wheels inside my head were spinning. "You had a donut yesterday."

"Yeah, so? What are you saying? I'm still pretty fit," Vance looked down at his waistline.

"I'm not judging your diet." I had to smile at that. "But what else did you eat?"

"All day? I have no idea."

"No, at the craft show. I've been trying to think of how the killer altered everyone's memory, and I think it might be with food. I know you had a donut, those chocolates from Christine, and the rock candy. Anything else?"

"I might've sampled one or two more things."

"How many, one or two?"

Vance seemed to think for a minute, counting the items off on his fingers. "Make that three, but I got the donut and the hotdog from the concession stand."

"We know the donuts came from Diane. I helped her carry them in. We can cross that off the list. And we know Aunt Thelma and Clemmie ate the chocolates, too. What else did you have?"

"Now you're really testing my memory." Vance stared into his coffee, lost in his thoughts. "I re-member pumpkin bread from Mrs. Potts and a glass of hot cider from Bonnie at the Tavern's table."

"I can't see how Bonnie or Mrs. Potts would have something to do with it. Maybe it's Christine. She was at the scene, and you did all eat the chocolate."

"And she is a former student of Lorraine's," Vance added.

"That could be our motive," I agreed.

"What we need is some evidence."

"I might know a way." I went on to explain that I had bought some chocolates from Christine and dropped them off at the inn as a treat for guests.

"What are you proposing? That you test them out on yourself?"

"Yes?" I couldn't keep the reluctance out of my voice.

"No, I don't like it."

"Do you have a better idea?"

"No, but that doesn't mean I won't think of one."

"Speaking of which, how is your memory?"

"Still some gaps, but I think most of it's there. I was wondering if Connie might be able—"

I didn't let Vance finish his thought. "That's a brilliant idea. If she has a potion to lift the mental fog, then I can try Christine's chocolates, and if it does affect my memory, I can just drink the potion."

Vance opened his mouth to protest, "That's not what I meant."

"No, but you have to admit it's a good plan. The best one we have. See, you were right. We would think of something better." I smiled encouragingly over the rim of my coffee cup. Vance looked dubious. I continued. "In the meantime, we still need to talk to Daniel and get a lead on his maker, and I got a hold of Lorraine's will. I never had a chance to talk to you about it last night, but Mayor Parrish met me at the courthouse. Together with Shelley Beaver, we found it, and I made a copy."

Vance looked at me expectantly. "I don't have it on me right now. I should have grabbed it, but the general gist is that Annabelle inherits everything. Oh! And I ran into Sally this morning. She told me that Annabelle hired her to be her father's nurse again."

"Sally was Mr. Springsdale's nurse?"

"Mm-hmm. She said Annabelle had to let her go when funds got tight, but now that she's rolling in the dough, she's rehired her—with a raise."

"So, how are Annabelle and Christine tied together?"

"I don't know. I don't see it. Annabelle gets the money, and what, Christine gets a cut?"

"We're operating under the assumption that Annabelle killed her mom, and now Christine is altering people's memories."

"Or, what if Annabelle killed her mom and cursed chocolates to frame Christine?"

"We don't know that the chocolates are cursed," Vance pointed out.

"Good point. So, we need to find that out for sure. I also think it wouldn't hurt to talk to Aunt

Thelma and Clemmie again just to make sure there isn't another avenue we're not exploring." As much as I'd like to sit in Diane's cozy bakery all morning speculating, it was time to head on out and put our theories to the test.

FIFTEEN

"You have that blood for me?" Connie asked when we walked into the potion shop. She was standing behind the counter at her cauldron. A green mist swirled about in the air, smelling heavily of spearmint.

"Unfortunately no, but I'm hoping you can help with something else." Vance went on to explain his symptoms and how it felt like his brain was in a fog.

"We think the killer or someone close to them is altering people's memories, so they don't remember key details from the crime."

"That's smart of them. I have to admit. Unfortunately for them, though, I know just the thing. I don't carry it in stock. It doesn't have a very long shelf life, so I'll need to mix it up. You mind coming back in about an hour or two?"

I looked at Vance. "No, we can do that."

"Yeah, that should work," he agreed.

"What are you making there?" I was careful not to get too close, but the minty vapors were doing a fine job of clearing my sinuses.

Vance must've agreed, too, because he next asked, "Is it a cold elixir?"

Connie's face broke into a wide grin. "It's mouthwash. I like mine to have a bit more of a bite to it."

"Ah," Vance said, seeming unsure of what else to say.

"Well, it smells refreshing."

"An added bonus," Connie agreed. "I'll start your potion next. I think it'll do the trick.

We left Mix It Up! and headed over to the high school.

"I feel like we need to make a list, write everything down," I said to Vance as I rode with him over to the high school.

"Use your phone," Vance suggested.

I did just that, opening the note-taking application. "We need to get the potion from Connie, check if the chocolates are cursed, and see if Aunt Thelma and Clemmie remember anything else."

My thumbs flew across the screen as I tapped the note out.

"And if they ate anything else."

"That's right. We also need to check if Annabelle has an alibi for Friday night."

"And if she's friends with Christine. Maybe your aunt would know?"

"Good idea, let's ask her when we get there."

The gym wasn't quite as packed as the day before. Mayor Parrish might not think that was a good thing, but at that moment, it was nice to have a bit of space to walk around. Christine wasn't at the chocolate table yet; she was probably still returning Vicki's dogs, but I recognized the same woman there as the day before. "Do you know who she is?" I motioned with my head to Christine's table.

"You don't recognize her?" Vance asked.

I scrutinized the woman a bit more but quickly looked away when she turned her gaze my way. I didn't want to get caught staring. "She looks vaguely familiar." The woman was older than Christine, closer to our age, which only made me all the more curious.

"That's Morgan Montgomery, formerly Morgan Taylor."

"No way, no, it's not." Morgan Taylor had platinum blonde hair and skin the color of honey, or at least that's what she looked like when I left Silverlake years ago. The woman before me had short auburn-colored hair and pale skin.

"She married Matt a couple of years after we left town. They have two girls now."

I took a closer look. "I guess I can see it, but man, I'd never put the two together if you hadn't told me."

"I know. She looks completely different. Matt told me she's working part-time at the library now that both of the girls are in school."

"I saw Matt Friday night. He was talking to Daniel outside of the school. Does he still play?" Vance had been back home for a few years while I was still trying to get caught up with what everyone had been up to.

"Not that I know of. Not any place public." Matt played guitar like Daniel, but he was never as strong a player, or maybe Matt never wanted to take center stage. It was hard to tell.

"I didn't think you two would stop by today." Aunt Thelma joined us.

"Morning. I wanted to check in with you." I looked around to make sure no one was eavesdropping. Aunt Thelma immediately caught on. "This is about the case, isn't it?" She kept her voice low. "Did you solve it?"

"What did they say?" Clemmie hollered over

Aunt Thelma's shoulder. She was sitting down at their table. Her arms folded across her chest and her legs stretched out before her. Aunt Thelma shot Clemmie a look, telling her to be quiet.

"First, what did you two eat yesterday?" I asked.

"You think someone cursed our food?"

"It's a theory," Vance said.

Not one to be left out, Clemmie stood up and joined us. I waited for Aunt Thelma to relay the information.

"Tell you what, I'm not eating anything today. I could taste that kettle corn all night long." Clemmie used the side of her fist to beat her chest.

Aunt Thelma grimaced. "I'm afraid we sampled quite a bit. We were here all day, and there were plenty of free samples."

"Did you have rock candy, hot cider, and a hot dog?" Vance asked.

Clemmie raised her hand. "I had some cinnamon raisin bread too. Now that was delicious."

"From Mrs. Potts?" I asked.

"She does make the best fruit bread," Aunt Thelma remarked.

I looked over at the older lady's table. Mrs. Potts wouldn't curse anyone on purpose. But it wouldn't be the first time she was unwillingly involved in a murder. As my eyes roamed the gym, I noticed that Minerva wasn't there. "Was Minerva here yesterday?" Her table still had several knitted sweaters and blankets stacked on top.

"I don't think so. Poor woman's too ashamed to show her face. Not that I blame her," Clemmie said.

I looked over to Vance. He read my mind. "You want to pay her a visit?"

"I think it would be a good idea. If anything, to let her know that she's not alone and we're here for her." I then thought back to the second reason for our visit. I dropped my voice even lower as I turned my attention back to my aunt and Clemmie. "Do you know if Annabelle and Christine are friends?"

"Annabelle and Christine?" Clemmie looked taken back.

"Not that I know of, but I suppose they could be. Christine worked with Lorraine quite a bit. They could have known one another from before Lorraine and Annabelle's falling out."

Clemmie leaned forward. "You think the two of them are in it together?"

"It's a theory." I shrugged my shoulders as I repeated Vance's words.

"They're not buddies as far as I know, but we'll let you know if we hear anything."

"Thanks, Aunt Thelma." I turned to walk

away. "Oh, I almost forgot. Connie, is working on a fog-lifting potion. We're supposed to stop back in an hour or so and pick it up."

"Be sure to save some for us," Clemmie replied.

"That's the plan," Vance remarked.

"In the meantime, let me know if you think of anything else," I added.

"Of course, dear," Aunt Thelma remarked at the same time Clemmie said, "Oh, you know we will."

Vance and I left Aunt Thelma and Clemmie to continue selling their goods and made our way over to Mrs. Potts's table. Thankfully, Mr. Whiskers was at home today.

"Vance, Angelica, so good of you to stop by." Mrs. Potts finished off a slice of her cinnamon raisin bread before turning her attention to Vance. "Are you back for more pumpkin bread? I told you it was good." She brushed her hands off one another.

"It was delicious, thank you," Vance replied in all honesty.

"Can we get a loaf of the pumpkin and the cinnamon raisin?" I asked.

Vance looked at me and raised his eyebrows. I replied with a smile. If we were going to check Christine's chocolates, we should also check Mrs.

Potts' bread. Not only that, but I thought it would be a sweet gesture to take a gift over to Minerva's house, provided it wasn't cursed. Thinking of Daniel's grandma, I then said, "Did Minerva ever come back this weekend?"

Mrs. Potts had been placing two wrapped loaves into a grocery bag when she stopped. "Oh no, it's awful what happened, isn't it? I stopped by her place last night, but she didn't answer even though her car was in the driveway. I can't imagine what she's feeling, well, I can a little bit, but it isn't quite the same." Mrs. Potts didn't need to go into detail. Both Vance and I knew what she was talking about from a previous case.

"Vance and I are going to pop over to pay her a visit. I'll let her know that you're thinking of her."

"Will you? I'd greatly appreciate it. I know she didn't like Lorraine, but the last thing she needed was for Daniel to kill her."

I was in the process of opening my purse to pay Mrs. Potts when I stopped short. "Minerva and Lorraine didn't get along?"

"Good heavens, no. Minerva blamed Lorraine for Daniel leaving home. And when it boils right down to it, probably for him turning into a vampire too."

"Really?" Vance cocked his head to the side.

"If Lorraine hadn't filled Daniel's head with

stardom, Minerva wouldn't have been alone all these years, or that's what she said the other night."

"What night?" Vance asked.

"Why, just this past Friday night." Mrs. Potts leaned in closer. "The day Lorraine died," she whispered.

"Wow, that is something." I tried to wrap up the conversation. I knew Vance was thinking the same thing as I was. We needed to talk to Minerva and quickly. I went back to fetch the money out of my wallet, and that's when I remembered that my cash was missing. "Oh no, that's right, I lost my money."

"You lost your money?" Vance looked skeptical. He knew it wasn't like me to forget where I put my cash.

"It's missing from my wallet. I have no idea where it went." I confessed, leaving it at that.

"You know, there's a pickpocket going around," Mrs. Potts said.

"Is there now?" I replied as if I didn't already know.

Mrs. Potts nodded her head solemnly. "I'm not carrying any cash around with me. I'm going right from here to home."

"That's a smart idea," Vance agreed.

"Thanks for letting me know, and you stay safe too," I said.

"You lost your money?" Vance asked as we weaved back out of the gym.

"You know I didn't. I'm pretty sure it was stolen, but I have no idea how or when."

"I did too."

"What? When?"

"This morning. I noticed it at the bakery."

"Which was packed."

Neither one of us said a word for a moment.

"Did you stop anywhere else?"

"I didn't see anyone else except for Sally in the parking lot, and she was busy with the girls. They were arguing. Something about a cloak?" Vance wasn't sure.

I nodded. "They were doing the same when I ran into them."

"It's not Sally, which means it has to be someone in the bakery, but who?"

"Million dollar question," I replied. Yet another one we couldn't answer.

With our bread in tow, and our minds swirling yet again, we left the high school, saying goodbye to Aunt Thelma and Clemmie on our way out.

SIXTEEN

"We need to head over to Minerva's." Vance took the words right out of my mouth.

"But first, let's stop back in to see Connie. Maybe she has the potion ready." It was no use taking Minerva over a cursed loaf of cinnamon raisin bread. I was going to say as much to Vance when he popped a piece of the bread in his mouth.

"Hey! Are you crazy? After giving me grief about case-testing Christine's chocolate?"

Vance shrugged his shoulders as he swallowed. "First of all, I don't mind being a guinea pig. It's you who I don't want to see hurt. Second, we know Mrs. Potts' bread is fine. She was eating it when we approached the table, and she remembered everything from Friday night."

"Meaning her bread's not cursed."

Vance tapped his temple with his index finger. "Now you're thinking."

"I guess next stop, Minerva's."

Mrs. Potts was right, Minerva's sedan was in her driveway when we arrived, but other than that, there were no signs that she was home. Someone had drawn her windows tight, and seeing that it was daylight, it was impossible to know if any lights were on inside.

I opened Minerva's glass storm door and knocked on the wooden door inside. Minerva's jingle bell wreath jangled when my hand made contact. Vance and I stepped back, waiting to see if she would answer. For added measure, Vance leaned forward and rang the doorbell.

After a minute or two, it was apparent that Minerva wasn't going to come to the door. We both stepped back off the porch and admired the house from the entryway sidewalk.

"Do you think she skipped town?" I whispered, unsure why I was doing so.

"If she killed Lorraine, it's a possibility."

"But would she leave her grandson to take the fall?" That didn't seem likely, and why would she set it up to make it look like a vampire bite in the first place?

"That's why we need to find her."

"What do you want to do?" Breaking and entering wasn't in my skill set, and I didn't want it to be. Sheriff Reynolds and his daughter would love any excuse to arrest me.

Vance walked over to the detached garage and peered inside the window. Coming up empty, he continued to walk around Minerva's garage, checking the side door, and then went to knock on Minerva's back door.

"Vance, duck!"

I wasn't sure what possessed me to yell, and it must've been my cat-like reflexes, but thank goodness Vance listened to me. The two of us hit the ground at the same time. A curse flew right past Vance's shoulder and hit the driveway instead. Red sparks rained down from behind Minerva's wooden privacy fence. Whoever was back there didn't want us to come any closer. Vance scrambled to his feet, and I did the same. Keeping low to the ground, we ran back to his truck and took cover behind the truck bed.

"What the heck is going on?" Vance asked as he drew his wand. I did the same, ready to counterattack if it came to it.

"Sorry! Sorry!" Minerva opened the latch of

her gate and came hobbling out. The old lady was dressed head to toe in black, including a black stocking cap and black eye grease smudged under her eyes. Vance and I both stood there dumbstruck.

"I thought you were that reporter again from Witch News Network coming to hound me again. She won't give me a moment's peace, so it's time that I fought back."

"Stormy Evans?" I guessed. I hadn't heard she was in town.

"Don't even say her name." Minerva practically growled.

"And here we thought we were coming to rescue you," Vance quipped as we walked up the driveway, meeting Minerva at her back door.

"I don't need to be rescued. What I need is to be left alone," Minerva grumbled.

"Pumpkin bread?" I offered up, hoping I hadn't beaten the loaf up too much in our quick retreat.

"Mrs. Potts?" Minerva asked.

"The one and only. She asked us to send her regards."

Minerva opened the door for us to follow her in. "I don't know what that reporter thinks I could tell her. I didn't see a thing. And I already told her Daniel's innocent, but did she want to hear that? No." Minerva put on a pot of coffee even though

she didn't ask if we wanted any and set about getting three mugs down. While the coffee perco-
lated, Vance and I took a seat at the kitchen table.
Minerva continued to fuss about, getting out the
cream and sugar followed by a stack of dessert
plates. The scene was something else, given the
woman's recon ensemble.

When it didn't seem like Minerva was going to
offer up any other info, I said, "But you must have
some idea who had it out for Lorraine."

Minerva slid a knife out of the butcher block
and turned around to face us. She raised the knife
at eye level and pointed forward.

I scooted back in my chair. Vance looked
about the room, possibly for a weapon.

Minerva read our expressions and shook her
head, putting the knife down. "Aren't you guys
jumpy. I was only going to cut the bread." Minerva
brought the bread over to the knife. "I'm going to
assume you heard that I don't like Lorraine based
on that reaction."

Vance cleared his throat. "That might have
been brought up once or twice."

"Whoever told that to you isn't lying. I didn't
care for Lorraine. And, contrary to what most
people believe, it started long before she was ever
Daniel's music teacher." Minerva paused for dra-
matic effect.

"Is that so," I replied because really, it's what she wanted to hear.

"Lorraine rubbed me the wrong way. You could tell she only cared about what others could do for her. If you were going to be somebody, she wanted to be a part of it. The minute you couldn't benefit her, she dropped you and moved on to the next person."

"She used people," I summarized.

"That's the word for it. People like her have no place in my life. I mean, look at what she said to Daniel Friday night? She adored my grandson. Then," Minerva snapped her fingers, "the next second, she hated his guts. Who does that?"

"I bet that made you angry," Vance said cautiously.

"Don't you try your reverse psychology on me. I watch Dateline. I know all about how investigators get confessions. I'm telling you, my conscience is clear. What I want to know is why Sheriff Reynolds isn't willing to investigate this case. He does realize that you can make any stab wound look like a vampire bite, doesn't he? Heck, I could even do it with my knitting needles if they were sharp enough."

I thought about Minerva's remark momentarily but then decided to play devil's advocate. "It's more than that, though. Don't you think it's

suspicious I saw Daniel running away from Lorraine's body, and the two of them had fought
earlier?"

"Sure, I'll give you that." Minerva sunk the
knife through the dense bread, cutting it into an
inch-thick slice. She plated the piece on a white
ceramic dish before repeating the task. "But
Daniel's no killer, vampire or not, and he's not the
only person Lorraine fought with." Minerva had a
wicked glint to her eyes.

"I thought you said you didn't have anything
else to tell Stormy Evans?"

"Like she wants the truth." Minerva sighed in
frustration. "But I tried to tell Sheriff Reynolds
that Lorraine got into a fight with Mr. Powell
Friday night too. It was right when we were setting up early in the evening. I couldn't make out
all the details, but it looked like he was grilling
hotdogs for the concession stand, and she was
ranting and raving about something or other. I
didn't pay any attention at the time, but now?
Now it's worth looking into."

I looked over at Vance, and I could tell he
wanted to head back over to Mr. Powell's house as
much as I did.

"In any way, I know you don't think Daniel's
guilty, or else you wouldn't be here right now."
Minerva handed a plate of bread to each of us and

then turned around to fill our coffee mugs. "Cream or sugar?"

Vance and I relayed our preferences.

"You're right. We don't think Daniel's guilty," Vance said, taking the mug from Minerva.

"That's why he came back into town. I know he didn't get a chance to talk with you, but he was hoping you could help him get turned back into a witch."

"He what now?"

"There's a potion that can change you back —" I started to say.

"I know about the potion," Minerva shook her head, telling me that that was old news. "Why didn't he say something right away? He can drink the potion, turn himself back, and prove his innocence. Case closed." Minerva said.

Technically, it wouldn't be case close, not even close. But Daniel would be innocent and free of charges. I didn't say that, though.

"We're working on it," it was Vance who spoke up.

"We have to stop by and see Daniel and find out who the vampire is that changed him."

Minerva looked off into the distance. "You need their blood."

Vance and I nodded. I was surprised by how much Minerva knew about the reversal spell.

"It was a long time ago. Don't ask," she added.

I tried not to look at Vance, but I knew he was thinking the same thing. Had Minerva been turned into a vampire at one time or another? If not her, then someone close to her.

"Right then." I wasn't sure what else to say. I cleared my throat. "Anyway, we're working the case from multiple angles right now. While we track down Daniel's maker, we're also trying to find out who the real killer is. If you were us, do you think you'd go back and question Mr. Powell?"

"That's what I told Sheriff Reynolds. His daughter Amber was with him. Can you believe that that girl had the audacity to roll her eyes at me?"

Yeah, I could believe it. Amber was snarky that way. "She was lucky I didn't wipe that smug expression off her face with my wand. If Daniel wasn't already in enough hot water, I think I would've done it."

I leaned across the table. "And I would've liked to have seen it."

Minerva smiled a wide grin. It might have only lasted a second, but in that one moment, she looked happy, and I vowed that the lady would be smiling every day sometime soon.

"We're not getting anywhere," I said to Vance once we were back in his truck. "We have Mr.

Powell and Lorraine fighting, Annabelle set to inherit, and she just rehired Sally as a nurse, and don't forget we still don't know who's cursing everyone."

"Or who Daniel's maker is."

"Gah, that's right. We should probably go there next."

"I agree."

SEVENTEEN

"So, do you want the good news or the bad news first?" Vance asked as we sat with Daniel in one of the interview rooms. The room was shoebox-size with pale white walls. A small table with four chairs filled the space. A black security camera with a steady red light stared down at us from the corner of the room.

"I guess the good news." Daniel sat back and folded his hands below the table. He was wearing a county commissioned blue jumpsuit since the Sheriff took his clothes as evidence. The moment I saw Daniel in his jail garb, a lump formed in my throat. It was just wrong with what was happening to Daniel. It made me feel sad and sick to my stomach at the same time.

"That's what I would go with too. The good news is that Angie found the reversal spell."

"You did? That's great!" Daniel's eyes lit up with excitement. He looked like he wanted to jump up and hug me but thought better of it. As it was, his fangs had descended in a rush of adrenaline, no doubt.

"But what's the bad news?" Daniel directed the question to me.

"We need the blood of the vampire who changed you." I delivered the news as calmly as possible. Perhaps the vampire was a friend of Daniel's and it wouldn't be a big deal at all.

"Oh man, you have to be kidding me. That chick is crazy! Like, you don't understand, she's nuts." Daniel enunciated each word. "I don't even know where to find her. I don't want to find her. I don't want you to find her either. I mean, if she changed me without any warning, I can't imagine what she'd do to you. You either," Daniel said, looking at Vance. The joy that had filled his face moments ago was gone completely.

"I was afraid of that," I replied under my breath.

"Why don't you back up a bit. Who is this girl?" Vance asked.

Daniel shook his head. "Man, Gran always

said a woman was going to be the death of me. I doubt she thought it would happen like this."

"She was an ex-girlfriend then?" I tried to make sense of what Daniel was saying.

"Not even. I met her after one of our concerts, just one night. That's all it took."

"In New Orleans?" Vance asked.

"Yep, good old Nola. It's not like I'm totally innocent, don't get me wrong. The guys and I like to let loose after shows. We were at an after-party thrown by a local radio station. A bunch of people were all around. Drinks were flowing, and music was pumping when this girl strikes up a conversation with me. At first, I thought she was just a cool girl. I didn't even know she was a vampire. I guess that tells you how drunk I was." Daniel looked at us as if he was there, desperate for us to believe his story.

"Then what happened?" I asked. Any clues Daniel could provide us would help us track her down.

"She told me her name was Victoria. We hit it right off. We talked about everything, even coming here to Silverlake. She told me she'd vacationed here dozens of times. Like I said, I thought she was a witch. I didn't see the fangs until it was too late." Vance and my expression must've looked skeptical because, in the next moment, Daniel said, "I don't know, maybe she glamoured me. I heard vampires can do that. You know, make you do whatever they want you to do. They put you under their spell. I've never done it. I'm not even going to try." Daniel held up his hands in surrender. "The point is, I later found out that she's a stalker fan. Completely obsessed with the band. She claims to be in love with me and knows everything about me. Everything. My favorite food, shoe size, where I grew up, the guitar I play, favorite ice cream. One minute she seemed super cool, and the next, her fangs are on my neck, and it was too late. After that, it was lights out. When I woke up, my world was rocked."

"And you haven't talked to her since?" Vance asked.

"No, but she's called my phone a hundred times. I can't even tell you how many text messages she's sent."

"You have her phone number?" Finding Victoria was going to be easier than I thought.

"I don't have it anymore. Sheriff Reynolds took my phone."

I looked at Vance. I knew as Daniel's attorney that he could request phone records. I wondered if that was still the case and how long it would take to get Victoria's number. Hopefully not long.

Vance looked over at me. "We should be able to get it," he confirmed.

I nodded. "You read my mind."

Thank heavens for small favors and deputies who cared about discovering the truth.

"Give me a little bit of time," Deputy Jones said when Vance asked him for Victoria's number.

"Thanks. Call me as soon as you have it," Vance said on our way out.

After leaving the sheriff's department, we drove over to the potions shop, and thankfully Connie had the fog-lifting potion corked up and ready to go.

"Perfect timing." Connie held the bulb-shaped bottle up to the sunlight streaming through the front window and examined the contents. Inside the glass was a clear blue potion. It looked like blue raspberry soda as effervescent bubbles rose to the surface.

"Make sure to keep it corked. It goes flat pretty quickly, and once it loses its fizz, it's worthless." Connie handed the potion to Vance.

Vance pulled out the cork and took a swig.

"Careful there," Connie remarked, reaching

with her hand to stop Vance before he drank anymore.

"Whoa." Vance staggered backward. His eyes became as wide as saucepans.

"Are you okay?" I looked to Vance and then Connie to gauge how concerned I should be.

Vance squeezed his eyes shut and sucked in a breath.

Connie reached forward, took the bottle out of Vance's hand, and safely pushed the cork back in. At the same time, I steadied Vance, placing my hand on his elbow.

"That hurts, wow," Vance looked pained.

"The potion?" I asked. Maybe Connie didn't mix it up right.

"I think he means the memories," Connie said softly.

"She would be correct." Vance cracked open an eye and pointed his finger at Connie. He closed his eye and took a deep breath in through his nose and out through his mouth, resting his head between his hands in the process.

"You okay?" My voice was a mere whisper.

Vance took a couple more deep breaths before responding. "There are some things a man doesn't want to remember." Connie and I looked at one another, but neither one of us said anything. Vance clearly didn't want to talk about it.

Instead, I switched to safer memories. "Does that mean you remember everything from yesterday now?"

Vance opened his eyes and blinked as if the sunlight seemed harsher than it had moments ago. "You could say that. That's some potion you've got there," Vance said the second part to Connie.

"You didn't wait for me to give you the directions. Be glad you're still standing," Connie quipped.

"You're right. My fault." Vance moved to massage his forehead with his fingertips. Dropping his hand, he looked at me with the full intensity of his startling blue eyes and something more. It was a look that took my breath away. "I'm sorry I missed our date. I can't believe I forgot it." Connie looked away. I gulped because when your boyfriend looks at you like that, it makes your tummy get tingly and your heart well up in your throat.

I took a steadying breath. "It's not your fault," I managed to say. I switched the conversation to safer ground. "Do you remember anything else?"

"Like, do I suddenly know who killed Lorraine?" I nodded hopefully. "Ah, no." Vance rubbed the back of his neck with the palm of his hand, clearly still dealing with the effects of the potion. "I'm not sure why I was targeted or if I even was."

"You think you were at the wrong place at the wrong time?" Connie asked, rejoining our conversation.

"I'm beginning to think so," Vance replied.

At that moment, the front door to Connie's shop opened, and Luke stepped in. He took one look at our trio and stopped short. "Are you okay?" Luke directed the question to Vance.

"I look that good, huh?" Vance closed his eyes once more.

"What did you give him?" Luke looked to Connie and me.

"Don't blame them. It's my fault. A word to the wise, ask for the directions before you throw back a potion."

Luke chuckled. "I could've told you that, man." He clapped Vance on the back.

"What can I do for you?" Connie asked, leading Luke away.

From behind us, I heard Luke mention my name and something about relaxation tonics and a Christmas present for his sister.

"Are you sure you're alright?" I searched Vance's face.

"I am." Vance looked away, and I didn't believe him for a second. I was debating if I should pry further when Vance turned back to me. "Remember that awful day thirteen years ago when you gave me back the engagement ring and left Silverlake?" It was my turn to wince. "That's the memory that hit me when I drank the potion." Suddenly Vance's soul-stirring look started to make sense.

"Vance." I reached out and took his hand in mind. I didn't know what else to say. Nothing else needed to be said. The fact that we'd found our way back to one another was enough.

Vance lifted my hand to his lips and kissed the space just above my knuckles. If we weren't in the middle of the potions shop, I would've melted into a puddle right there and made a sappy fool of myself. Vance lowered my hand but didn't let go.

"I'm glad I found you again," he said.

"I'm glad I found me again, too."

"You two doing okay over there?" Connie asked from over by the register.

I blushed but managed to reply, "Never better."

As I looked over at Vance, a slow smile spread across his lips. Even though we were neck-deep in an investigation, I felt like the luckiest witch in the world.

EIGHTEEN

"Do you want to go back to the inn?" Vance asked as we pulled away from Village Square.

"That makes the most sense, and it's right here." I prayed that the guests hadn't eaten all the chocolates and that they weren't cursed. I'd feel awful if I inadvertently hexed my guests. My brow furrowed in concern.

"I'm sure everything's going to be okay," Vance said, reading my expression.

"I hope so. I'm not sure how I'm going to explain to the guests if the chocolates are cursed." I could only imagine how scathing the online reviews would be. Aunt Thelma and I had worked hard to build up Mystic Inn's reservation log. I didn't want to see all of our hard work be in vain.

"Who says you have to tell them?" Vance looked at me and quirked his brow.

"I cannot believe you said that."

"Hear me out. People come on vacation to relax. All you did was make them forget their problems for a day or two. They'll probably think it's the greatest vacation ever."

I looked skeptical. "I don't know."

"Well, I do. Who knows, it might be an added service you offer. Come to Silverlake and forget your troubles." Vance held his right hand out, palm up while he spoke, pretending to be an announcer. He held onto the steering wheel with his other hand.

I shook my head.

"All I'm saying is it might not be such a bad thing."

I thought for a moment, looking at the situation as a whole. "No, you're right. If the chocolates are cursed, that means Christine is the killer, and the case is closed." Or nearly closed, and that was what was more important. I was banking on getting Victoria's blood to change back Daniel. Once we proved he was innocent, Sheriff Reynolds would have to look at the rest of the evidence. I was sure that if Christine were the killer, we would just have to dig a bit deeper to find the means and the motive.

"You think Victoria's going to help Daniel willingly after he dumped her?"

"I wouldn't say that he dumped her. It's more like he dropped off the face of the earth."

"And that makes it any better?"

"It was an extenuating circumstance. And remember, it's not like they were dating. This all happened on one night. One crazy, wild night."

"Wild, indeed."

"But to get back to your question, I have no idea how Victoria's going to react. I have an idea, and I'm not sure it's going to work, and I think you're going to think I'm crazy."

Vance turned into the parking lot of the inn and pulled into a parking space. Vance shifted the car into park and turned to face me. "Now you have my attention."

I swallowed nervously. I hadn't thought my plan out all the way through. It was more like a vague idea. "Here's what I'm thinking. We text Victoria and pretend to be Daniel. She knows that he's a vampire, or she has a pretty good guess. We ask her to come to Silverlake, and then when she gets here, we intercept. This is where it gets a bit dodgy." And where Vance would object, rightfully so. I cleared my throat. "I'm thinking that if we can't reason with her, then maybe we can use force."

"You want to set up a trap for Victoria."

I looked down at my lap, not meeting Vance's eyes. "I know vampires are dangerous, deadly even, and it's not a smart plan, and —"

"I think it's brilliant."

My lips parted with shock. "You do?" I was not expecting that.

"I don't see how else we're going to do it. If we get Victoria to come to Silverlake, at least we can have backup should it come to that."

"Really? Okay. I thought for sure you wouldn't agree."

"No, I'm all for the plan. I don't want you any-where near Victoria when it goes down. But if you want to send the text, I'm all for it."

"Hey, now, it's my idea."

"Do you really want to be at ground zero when a vampire finds out that she's been lied to?"

I thought twice. "Not really," I confessed. Ap-parently, my need for self-preservation trumped my desire to be a hero.

"Let me talk to Deputy Jones. Give some guys on the force a heads up with what we're planning and see if they can help."

"You're right. That's better than me jumping out and yelling boo!"

"I'll talk to the deputy when he calls with Victoria's number."

Vance and I got out of his truck and walked into the lobby. It was quite the social scene with several guests mingling about. A couple was cozied up on the couch in front of the fire, glasses of wine sitting before them on the coffee table. A young family was seated around the dining table playing a board game. A solo traveler was kicking it back in one of the side chairs. His legs stretched out in front of him with his laptop resting comfortably on his lap. Percy floated above, with a Santa hat upon his head, refilling wine glasses and passing out bowls of popcorn. Kyle, another weekend helper, was behind the registration desk checking in another arrival.

"This place is hopping." Vance took the words out of my mouth.

It might not be hopping compared to big city hotels, but this was as busy as Mystic Inn ever got, and it felt so warm and cozy, and so much like home, that I couldn't stop the broad smile that filled my face.

My eyes roamed the counter, and I spotted the platter of chocolates from yesterday. I was relieved to see that quite a few were left. Kyle was just extending his hand to offer a chocolate to Mr. and Mrs. Leighton, our newest guests when I snatched the glass plate from the counter. "Sorry, I was just going to top it off a bit," I said, whisking the plate away. From behind me, I heard Kyle falter as he tried to cover my social faux pas, mumbling something about candy canes available on the lobby's Christmas tree.

Vance followed after me, and we ducked inside the inn's small, ground-level kitchen. The space was used primarily as a breakfast prep area and a place to keep treats for guests. Aunt Thelma kept the fridge stocked with fresh, cut-up fruit and juices, and Diane's bakery provided baked goods throughout the week. It was also where the wine fridge was located, which allowed guests to buy wine or champagne by the glass or bottle. Not to mention the cupboard was full of all sorts of goodies like chips, popcorn and candy. You never knew when the inn would host a movie night or set up a hot chocolate bar like the night before.

I slid the glass plate onto the counter and took my purse off my shoulder so that I could retrieve the potion, which I'd safely tucked inside. In the two seconds it took me to grab the bottle, Vance bit into one of the chocolates.

"Will you quit doing that!" I glared at my boyfriend.

Vance was unable to reply, given the amount

of chewing the caramel-filled chocolate had required.

"I was going to taste the chocolates, remember? We can't have you losing your memory, getting it back, and losing it again. That can't be good for anyone," I continued to lecture.

Vance sucked the caramel off his teeth. "Sorry, I forgot."

I glared at Vance. "No, you didn't."

"Maybe my memory's still not all there," Vance smiled.

"You are incorrigible."

"I'm not even sure what that means, but thank you."

An awkward moment of silence passed before I asked, "How do you feel? Do you remember what we're doing here?"

"You mean other than me trying to be chivalrous and you lecturing me on my gentlemanly pursuit."

"Okay, so your memory is still there."

"I don't feel any different," Vance confirmed.

"Wonder how long it would take?"

"I don't know."

I watched the seconds tick by on the clock.

"Still nothing?"

"Still nothing. I say we carry on."

"Well, that was a bit of a disappointment." I

didn't want Christine to be the killer or my guests to be cursed, but I hated knowing a killer was running around our community, and I was powerless to find them.

I left the chocolates in the kitchen to be on the safe side and said goodbye to Kyle on our way out the door. I was sure he wondered what happened to the chocolates, but I didn't give him a chance to ask.

"Where to, boss?" Vance asked once we buckled in.

"What do you think? Swing by Mr. Powell's to find out more about his fight with Lorraine or head to Annabelle's for her alibi?"

"How about Mr. Powell first and then Annabelle?" Vance suggested.

"That sounds good to me."

It turned out it didn't matter whose house we went to first because Mr. Powell wasn't home.

"He's probably back at the craft show, no?" Vance asked.

"I don't know. I didn't see him there this morning. We can double-check when we head back, though. I still want to get Aunt Thelma and

Clemmie the potion and see if it helps them remember anything."

When we arrived at Annabelle's, she was assisting her dad in getting into the car. She had pulled his wheelchair up to the car door and was positioning Mr. Springsdale in the front passenger seat. I suddenly felt like the worst sort of witch for asking Annabelle for her alibi. Seeing the way she tenderly cared for her father, tucking a red flannel blanket around his legs before shutting the door to see to his wheelchair, made me rethink our visit.

"Sweet scorpions! You two scared me!" Annabelle startled when she looked up, and her eyes locked with mine. Anger flashed in her eyes. I took a step back. Vance looked at me to see if I'd caught it. I nodded that I did.

Annabelle pushed the wheelchair to the back of the car, popped the trunk, and then turned to collapse the chair. "What can I do for you?" Her tone was brisk.

"Here, let me help you." Vance stepped forward to lift the chair and slide it into the trunk.

"Sorry for just dropping by unannounced, and I know you're busy," I started to say. Annabelle stood there and crossed her arms, waiting for me to get on with it. I cleared my throat. "I was just wondering if you had a chance to stop by the craft show." My courage failed me at the last moment.

"What?" Vance and Annabelle asked me at the same time.

"Okay, you're right. That wasn't what I was going to ask."

"What Angelica really wanted to ask is where were you Friday night, but she doesn't want to come across as insensitive." Vance gave me a sympathetic look.

"He's right," I confessed.

"You think I killed my mother? That's what this is about?" Annabelle was fuming. "You have to be kidding me. I wanted absolutely nothing to do with the woman. She wasn't worth the dirt on the ground. I wouldn't destroy my life to end hers. I can promise you that." Annabelle looked back at the car and her father inside.

"I don't know. You have a lot of anger," Vance said calmly. I wasn't sure if goading her was the best choice of action, but I left Vance to his tactic. "And we read the will," Vance motioned between him and me with his hand. "It looks like you're going to inherit quite a bit. Enough money to hire a nurse for your father. Maybe make your home more handicap accessible." Vance motioned to the front porch where a ramp should be. "That sounds like a motive to me."

"I'm not going to lie. The money's going to be nice. I can't believe she still left it to me. Although,

I have no idea who else she could've left it to. No-body likes her, not for long."

"Why did you go see Boyd about the will last month?" I cocked my head to the side.

Annabelle faltered. "How do you know about that?"

I shrugged. "Does it matter?"

Annabelle shot me a livid glare. I kept my expression impassive. "In case you hadn't noticed, my dad's health is failing." Annabelle kept her voice low. "I had a copy of my mother's will. I wanted to use it as a template to update his, but I wasn't sure if it was current or if I should use a different one." Annabelle swallowed uncomfortably. Tears formed in her eyes. She took a ragged breath.

"I'm sorry." I apologized.

Annabelle huffed, not believing me for a minute. "So, to answer your other question." Annabelle glared at me as she stuck her hand in her coat pocket. I instinctively reached for my wand in my back pocket. Annabelle pulled out a ticket stub and thrust it forward. "I took dad to a movie. It started at seven-thirty. Go ahead and check it out with the theater. I've got nothing to hide. Now, if you'll excuse me, we're going to be late." Annabelle brushed beside me and proceeded to get to her car without another word. Vance and

I stepped back and allowed Annabelle to back down the driveway. I waved at them both as they passed. Mr. Springsdale returned the gesture with a warm smile and a head nod.

"At least one of them is friendly," Vance remarked. "Still want to confirm her alibi?"

"It would probably be a good idea. But first, let's head back to the high school."

NINETEEN

It was the final push in the craft show, and the morning lull had all but disappeared. We found ourselves parking further out and making the walk into the gym. Vance held my hand as we weaved in between cars and then over to the sidewalk that ran along the parking lot and up to the high school.

I smelled the charcoal before I spotted Mr. Powell. Vance motioned with his head toward the grill. Someone had set it up outside the side door of the gym, which was convenient to the concession stand. I faltered when I took in Mr. Powell's appearance, momentarily coming to a standstill. I quickly recovered and shuffled forward.

"Vance, look what's in his hand," I whispered.

It was a grilling fork. The utensil was over a foot long with a wooden handle and prongs that could leave a nasty wound, a wound that would look an awful lot like a vampire bite. "It could be the murder weapon."

"You're right. We should've looked for one sooner."

"What do we do?"

Vance smiled at Mr. McCormick as he walked towards us with Matt Montgomery. The men gave a head nod and said hello as they passed. Vance did the same in return. I tried to smile back, but given the concerned look on Mr. McCormick's face as he passed by, I was convinced I'd failed miserably. Vance was doing a far better job of keeping his cool than I was.

"Here's what we're going to do," Vance said when it was just the two of us walking again. "You go in and give the potion to Thelma and Clemmie, and I'll wait until Mr. Powell goes back inside and nab the fork. I'll meet you back at my truck in ten minutes."

"Okay, then what?" We might be jumping to conclusions, but I couldn't shake the suspicion that the grilling fork was important.

"Then we'll take the fork to Deputy Jones and see what he thinks."

I exhaled and felt a nervous shudder move

through me. We had to be getting close to solving this case. We just had to be. Vance squeezed my hand before letting go. I continued forward into the school while he veered off to the left.

"Oh!" Aunt Thelma said when I approached her table. "You're surprising me left and right today, dear. I didn't think I'd see you yet again."

"Look in her eyes. She's on to something, I can tell." Clemmie said, joining my aunt.

"I think we might be, which is why I can't stay. I only wanted to drop Connie's potion off." I retrieved the bottle from my bag and discreetly handed it over to my aunt. "Make sure you only take a sip. A very small sip," I clarified.

"That potent, huh?" Clemmie eyed the bottle suspiciously.

"Use the potion and then call me and let me know if you remember anything from Friday night," I instructed.

Clemmie saluted me like a soldier.

"Make sure to call us too," Aunt Thelma said.

"Yeah, don't leave us in the dark," Clemmie added.

"Don't worry. I won't. We'll talk soon."

When I got back to the truck, Vance was already sitting inside with the engine running and ready to go.

"You got it?" I climbed in and shut the door.

Vance nodded, and I noticed that he was no longer wearing his coat. "It's on the backseat." I peered over my shoulder and saw Vance's coat bundled around a long object. "I didn't want to touch it with my bare hands."

"That's a good idea."

"And I think you're right. It looks like there is dried blood under the handle."

"Are you kidding me?" It seemed my instincts might be paying off.

It felt like it took an exceptionally long time to drive over to the sheriff's department, even though it couldn't have been more than ten minutes.

Vance called Deputy Jones when we pulled into the parking lot and put his phone on speaker.

"Deputy Jones," the man said when he picked up his end of the line.

"Hey, Deputy. It's Vance and Angelica."

"You must be a mind reader. I was about to give you a call."

"You have Victoria's number?" Vance asked.

"I do, and Daniel didn't lie. This girl is obsessed with him. Ninety-seven missed phone calls and two hundred text messages. I hope you know what you're doing."

"So do I." Vance looked at me. "Listen, that's not why I'm calling, or not the only reason. We may have found the murder weapon. I wasn't sure how you wanted me to proceed."

"You what now?" The sound of a metal drawer sliding open and then shut interrupted the conversation as if the deputy was looking for something to write with.

"We're here in the parking lot. We found it at the high school. I used my coat to pick it up because, well, it's a bit of a long story. Do you want me to bring it in?"

"No, I'm on my way out."

Deputy Jones came jogging down the department's front steps with a brown paper bag tucked under his arm. Vance and I got out of the truck and met the deputy by the driver's side door. Vance opened the back door and motioned to his coat. "It's a grilling fork. Mr. Powell was using it to roast hot dogs when Angelica and I spotted it."

Deputy Jones put on a pair of gloves and reached for Vance's coat, unwrapping the fork.

"If you look closely, there's dried blood under the wood handle." Vance pointed it out.

Deputy Jones examined the fork and nodded his head. "I think you're right. You shouldn't have picked it up though. You should have left it at the scene."

"We know, but Mr. Powell was using it, and

we didn't want him to know that we are on to him," I tried to explain.

"You think Mr. Powell is the killer?"

"He could be. He was dating Lorraine, which I didn't know about. And Minerva? She said she overheard Lorraine and Mr. Powell fighting Friday night. She told Sheriff Reynolds, but I don't think he looked into it. Do you?"

"Not that I know. Sheriff still thinks Daniel is his man."

"About that. Angelica has an idea, but we want to run it by you," Vance said.

We spent the next ten minutes talking about tricking Victoria into coming to town.

Deputy Jones looked concerned. "You realize Sheriff Reynolds will fire me on the spot if he finds out you invited another vampire to town, and I knew about it and didn't stop you, right?" I hadn't thought of it that way. Deputy Jones was right, of course. I was asking him for a lot. "But, if what you're saying is true, and I believe it is, it's the right thing to do. If we're going to get the sheriff to believe anyone else is guilty, we're going to have to change Daniel back into a witch, first."

I exhaled. "So, you'll help us?"

"I suppose, when is she coming?"

"Hand over her number, and I'll text her right away." I held out my hand. Deputy Jones reached into his pocket and passed over a slip of paper. I unfolded the small piece of paper and looked at the ten-digit number.

"Let's hope this works." I opened my text messages and punched in the number on my phone. "Hey, it's Daniel," I spoke aloud while texting. "I need your help. Can you come to Silverlake as soon as possible?" I left the message at that. Daniel said Victoria had been here dozens of times, so she should know how to enter the enchanted town. "Okay, I hit send. Now let's see if she replies."

Deputy Jones took Vance's coat and the fork and carefully placed them in a large brown paper bag. "Let me know what she says, and in the meantime, I'll send this to the lab."

After thanking Deputy Jones yet again (really, you can't thank a person enough for putting their career on the line), we swung by the movie theater. Not surprisingly, Annabelle had been telling the truth. More than one employee remembered seeing her with her dad Friday night, and they had stayed the entire time with their movie not ending until almost ten o'clock.

"So, maybe it is Mr. Powell then," Vance said as we walked back to his truck for the umpteenth time that day. We'd crossed Annabelle and Christine off the list, and Mr. Powell was the last person left.

"I don't know. Something about it doesn't sit right with me." The day was drawing to a close, and while we might have found the murder weapon and motive, I wasn't convinced Mr. Powell was our man. Short of a confession, I'm not sure what was missing. Maybe it was because I couldn't see Mr. Powell continuing to use the murder weapon. Not only was that gross, but it didn't make any sense. Wouldn't Mr. Powell have destroyed it or at the very least thrown it away? I explained my reservations to Vance.

"You're right. I can't see Mr. Powell leaving the murder weapon at the scene of the crime."

Both Vance and I were lost in our own thoughts. I was thinking that it might be time to widen the suspect pool and look at additional former students or maybe their family members. I wasn't even sure where to begin.

"Maybe we're thinking about this the wrong way." Vance's comment interrupted my thoughts.

"What do you mean?"

Vance was quiet for a moment while he seemed to gather his thoughts in order. "What if Lorraine wasn't the target. What if Daniel was?"

"You mean someone set him up?"

"That's what I'm thinking."

I ran with Vance's thoughts. "What if it's Victoria? What if she followed Daniel to Silverlake and framed him for murder just to get even?"

"Ouch, that's pretty—"

"Evil." I finished Vance's sentence. "I know."

"And a real possibility."

"I can't believe we didn't think of it before now."

"Me either. And even if it's not Victoria, there might be someone else in Silverlake who wanted revenge."

"Someone who held a grudge for the last decade and a half?" As far as I knew, Daniel hadn't been back in a long time.

"An ex-girlfriend?" Vance threw out there.

My eyes lit up. "Or, an ex-bandmate."

"Matt Montgomery."

"Right? Maybe it's him. He's stuck in Silverlake while Daniel hits it big. Think about it, Daniel dropped Matt after high school, and now he's stuck working what, at his dad's car dealership? Meanwhile, Daniel becomes a rock star. That had to hurt."

"And Morgan could be in on it, too," Vance said.

"She is working at the bizarre. Together they could have killed Lorraine and cursed any eyewitnesses."

"Okay, so we've opened a new theory that we need to look into more," Vance summarized.

"And not just Matt, but Daniel's past in general. There might be someone else that we're not even thinking about."

Vance and I drove back to the inn to continue our research.

While Vance ran a background check on Matt, I took a moment to reread Lorraine's will.

TWENTY

"I'm not finding anything on Matt or his wife," Vance said. "Their background checks are clean. No history of violence, very little debt. Neither one of them are very active on social media except posting pictures of their kids."

Vance and I were working from the front of the house. I would've liked to lock ourselves away in the inn's back office, but Percy had a date with Eleanor tonight, and Kyle had an exam to study for and asked if he could leave early. Thankfully, the lobby had quieted down as guests settled in for the night.

"You mean he didn't troll Daniel online?"

"Wouldn't that have been nice?"

"I'm looking at Lorraine's will. It is pretty

straightforward. The only thing is, I wonder how much some of these musical instruments are worth. She left a cello and necklace to her niece, a Miss Chloe Springsdale, and I don't know her at all."

"She's not from Silverlake," Vance agreed.

"And she left a violin to Christine and her piano to the high school."

"Hey guys," Emily said, walking through the front doors.

Vance and I looked up at Emily at the same time.

"Hey, what are you doing here?" I asked, surprised that she would drop in on a Sunday evening.

Emily looked sheepish. "Your aunt said I could stop by tonight and pick up my check instead of waiting till Tuesday. It's supposed to be in the office. I hope that's okay?"

"Oh, yeah. If Aunt Thelma said it's okay, it is. I'm sure she has it back there for you. Hang on, let me go check." I left Emily and Vance at the front desk and disappeared for a moment to retrieve the check. I know what I'd said to Emily, but I was surprised to find Emily's check exactly where it was supposed to be. I was proud of my aunt. Perhaps she was turning a new leaf. A witch could hope anyway.

"All the chocolates are gone again? Dang it, I was hoping for one of the caramel-filled ones. Those are my favorite," Emily remarked, noticing the plate was empty.

I walked back out and looked over at the chocolates. I hadn't even noticed they were back out. I didn't have a chance to comment because at that moment, my cell phone rang. I slipped the phone out of my pocket and saw that it was Aunt Thelma. "Hey, hang on a sec," I started to say to my aunt.

"Angelica? You have to come quick. It's an emergency!"

"Is this like the crafting emergency Friday night?" I shook my head to Vance and Emily, telling them not to worry. This was par for the course for my aunt.

"No, it's not like the crafting emergency," Aunt Thelma bit off. "Get to the high school —" There was a loud metal creaking sound and then the line went dead.

I froze as if someone had hit me with a glacio spell. I felt chilled to the bone.

"What's wrong?" Vance asked.

Emily, who'd been smiling at me moments ago, suddenly looked pale. "Are you okay?" she asked.

Common sense came rushing back to me. "We

have to go. Emily, can you watch the front? I'll get back as soon as I can." Emily barely had time to nod before I dragged Vance out the front door, explaining the phone call to him on the way.

Vance wasted no time, speeding out of the parking lot and racing toward the high school.

"What time is it anyway?" I asked as I looked at the clock on Vance's dashboard. In our quest to discover the truth, the rest of the evening had slipped away, turning into night. The high school parking lot was deserted except for a handful of scattered cars.

"Are you sure this is where she said she was?" Vance squinted, looking for any signs of Aunt Thelma.

During the ride over, I tried to convince myself to remain calm. "Maybe she was being melodramatic, and she locked her keys in her car, and her cell phone died," I said as Vance sped around the lake.

I held on to that thought until the last possible moment.

"I think so. I'm almost positive." I started second-guessing myself until I spotted Aunt Thelma's car and pointed it out to Vance. "She's still here."

Vance and I climbed out of his truck into the velvet darkness of night. It was a moonless night, causing the stars to appear brighter. In the distance, a dog barked. Vance and I both snapped our attention toward the sound before realizing what it was.

"Aunt Thelma?" I yelled into the darkness.

There was no response.

Vance and I walked over to her car and peered inside. She had it locked up tight with no sign of her purse or car keys in sight. So much for that theory.

With no sign of Aunt Thelma or Clemmie outside, we walked toward the school. The front door was still unlocked even though the inside lights were off.

I looked to my left and then right before proceeding to the gym. All of my instincts were on high alert. The tiger's eye around my neck glowed warm, reminding me that I was never alone and helpless. Powerful magic ran through my veins and would come to me if I called it. Vance withdrew his wand. Belatedly, I did the same.

Wands out and raised to attack, we crept forward. The trophy case cast an eerie glow onto the shadowed hallway and had me do a double-take more than once. It was a good thing I was more of the look-twice-shoot-once kind of witch. If not, I would've blasted the fire extinguisher into bits.

Peering into the gym, we saw that it was deserted. Every light was off, and every table and chair was put away. The booster club had even cleaned and shut down the concession stand, rolling down the blue metal door and securing it in place.

Wherever Aunt Thelma was, it wasn't here.

"Where do you want to go?" It would be quicker to split up and search, but not smarter.

"Where else would she be?" Vance replied.

I had no idea.

We began to methodically search the high school, going up and down halls and peering into darkened classroom doors.

"We should call for backup," Vance suggested.

"Good idea." It was a testament to how rattled I was that I hadn't thought of that sooner. Vance immediately got on the phone and called Deputy Jones, followed by Diane. Our friend would start the phone tree, and in no time, half the town would show up. I was sure of it.

We rounded the corner, and I almost walked directly into Mr. Powell.

"Mr. Powell," I said, scared out of my wits.

He had a large box in his arms, making it hard for him to see around it. For his part, the man looked as calm as can be.

"Wh-what are you doing?" My voice trembled. Vance was still on the phone with Diane but quickly hung up.

"Taking this box of handbells back to the band room. I thought I could find it well enough in the dark. What's the matter with you two?"

I looked at Vance. I had no idea what to say.

"Have you seen Thelma?" Vance asked.

"She was with Clemmie about a half-hour ago. I thought they left." Either Mr. Powell was a very good liar, or he was telling the truth. I wasn't sure which to believe. "Is everything okay?"

"I'm sure everything's fine. But if you see her, will you tell her I'm looking for her?" My words rushed out.

Mr. Powell gave me the oddest look. "Alright, I can do that. Well, you guys have a good night then."

"We will." I tried my best to smile as I grabbed Vance's hand and tugged him the opposite way down the hall. As soon as we rounded the corner, I stopped and took cover against the wall, pulling Vance with me.

"What are you doing?"

I put my finger to my lips to silence him and then peered around to see if Mr. Powell was still there.

He was gone.

"Come on, let's follow him."

Vance and I tiptoed back down the hallway, making sure not to come up too quickly on the band director, but stopped short when we passed by the choir room.

"What's going on in here?" Mr. Powell asked, flipping on the light.

"Don't look at me, ask her. She's the one that's lost her dang mind," Clemmie replied.

"This isn't supposed to happen!" Christine shrieked.

"You need to calm down. We can talk this through," came Aunt Thelma's voice.

I shot an alarmed expression at Vance. It sounded like Christine was holding Aunt Thelma and Clemmie hostage, and Mr. Powell walked right into the middle of it.

"Those two killed Lorraine," Christine said to Mr. Powell. "They were talking about it tonight," she lied, "and I overheard them."

"You what?" A fresh wave of grief appeared to wash over Mr. Powell. "Thelma? Clemmie? Why?"

"Don't listen to her whack-a-doodle. Use your brain, Carl. Why would we kill Lorraine?"

"I'm afraid she's lying, Carl. But why don't you call the Sheriff, and we'll let him sort this out," Aunt Thelma suggested.

"You can't do that," Christine replied. Her voice was deadly calm.

I held up my wand, "Stanzi on three," I whispered to Vance. I'd had enough of Christine. I wasn't going to sit around and wait for her to make her move. We were going to stun her into silence.

But before I could even mouth the word, chaos erupted. A swirling mass of darkness engulfed the room, snuffing out every ray of light and choking the air out with it.

I coughed, gasping for air. From beside me, Vance did the same. Instinctively, I hit the ground where the air was cleaner.

The black smoke stung my eyes, causing them to water.

From the corner of the room, the back door flew open, and Christine disappeared into the night.

I didn't wait. I gripped the stone around my neck and said the incantation to shift into my feline form, "Metamorfóno alithís ousía."

Suddenly my four paws were running at full speed, and I slipped through the metal door before it clicked shut.

The fresh nighttime air filled my lungs and propelled me forward. Christine couldn't have made it far.

Then I spotted her, running up ahead. She was running through the baseball field toward the forest. It was the same path Daniel had taken Friday night.

Only Christine wasn't going to get away.

My nails dug into the ground as I sprinted forward. I had no idea what I would do when I caught up with her, but she was not escaping, not after everything she'd done.

Second, by second, I drew up closer.

From behind me, I heard Vance and Mr. Powell. They were close behind, yelling for help and for Christine to stop.

I was almost within striking distance.

I threw all my power forward and leaped into the air, planning to land on Christine's back and sink my claws into her, when out of nowhere, a streak of red hair flew in from the side and crashed into us both.

We went down in a tangle of limbs and hair.

The breath was knocked out of me for the second time that night.

I scrambled to get out of the pile as the humans battled it out. It took a second to take in the scene.

Vance, Mr. Powell, Clemmie, and Aunt Thelma screeched to a halt.

A moment later, I realized why.

It was a vampire who'd taken down Christine.

It looked like Victoria had decided to come to town after all.

"Sorry about that," Victoria said, wiping her

hands off on her jeans. "Predatory instincts and all that. I couldn't help myself." She smiled, revealing her fangs in all her glory.

Clemmie crossed herself.

At that instant, I was more than happy to remain a cat.

Vance found his voice first. "No, thank you. You did the right thing."

Victoria cocked her head to the side, not following.

As much as I wanted to remain safely out of sight, I decided to morph back into human form and help explain what was going on, seeing my aunt and her friend seemed to have lost their voices.

Victoria did a double take as I seemed to appear out of nowhere. "I love magic," she said, taking in my appearance.

"Victoria, right?" I confirmed.

"Who are you?" Victoria's playful demeanor diminished, and the predator began to resurface.

"We're friends of Daniel's," I quickly explained.

"Well, except for her." Vance motioned to Christine.

She'd begun to inch away but froze solid when Victoria cast her hungry eyes her way.

"I'm the one that texted you because Daniel needs your help."

Victoria blushed. I didn't even know vampires could do that. "I know, I know, I shouldn't have bitten him. I love him so much. He's so incredible. Then when we hit it off, which I knew we were going to, and then one thing led to the other, and oh my gosh, where is he?" Victoria was in all-out fangirl mode. Her eyes darted around the high school grounds expectantly.

"What's going on over there?" Deputy Jones shined his flashlight our way.

"Don't even think about it," Vance said to Christine. His wand was raised and pointed at her. From behind him, Aunt Thelma and Clemmie glared at the woman.

Deputy Jones handcuffed Christine in short order. Sheriff Reynolds arrived on the scene shortly after, and even he couldn't ignore five direct witnesses.

"He needs my blood?" Victoria asked after the scene had died down.

"Only a little bit." I held up my thumb and index finger to measure out a pinch. At least, I thought it was only a little bit. Connie didn't actually say.

"Can I see him?" Victoria's eyes filled with

hope. I wasn't about to be the one to tell her otherwise.

"That's a good question. Why don't we stop by the potion shop first and then swing by the sheriff's department," Vance suggested.

I smiled broadly at Vance. His plan was brilliant.

"I'll call Connie now." It was late, and her shop was closed, but I knew she'd make a special exception. Now, if only I could think of what to get her for Christmas as a thank you. It was going to have to be something spectacular.

TWENTY-ONE

The following night the entire town stood around the giant fir tree at the center of Wishing Well Park, waiting for the tree lighting ceremony to begin. Mayor Parrish stood in front of the tree wearing a red wool coat and white fluffy hat that would make Mrs. Claus jealous with how warm and stylish it was.

Clemmie, Aunt Thelma, Vance, and I stood huddled together. I looked longingly at Mayor Parish's warm ensemble. Hopefully, we wouldn't be out here long.

"I still don't understand why Christine did it," Clemmie said, rubbing her hands together to stay warm.

"She had a lot of debt," Vance replied.

"A lot," I emphasized. "Lorraine convinced her to go to Harvardshire, but Christine couldn't afford it. She ended up taking out thousands of dollars in student loans, and even then, it wasn't enough. She had to drop out before graduating."

"With all that debt and no way to pay it back." Vance nodded.

"But why kill Lorraine. For revenge?" Aunt Thelma asked.

Vance answered that question. "Lorraine left Christine a Stradivari violin. They're worth thousands, even millions in some cases."

"My word," Clemmie and Aunt Thelma said at the same time.

"And the chocolates were cursed. Do you remember what Emily said last night?" I asked Vance.

He looked confused.

"She said the chocolates were gone again. When I checked with Emily today, she said the guests ate all the chocolates we put out. So, after seeing how much people enjoyed them, she put out a box she'd found in the kitchen cupboard."

"The chocolate I ate was one of those," Vance surmised.

"Exactly, and not one of Christine's. But you were right," I said to Vance.

"Naturally," Vance replied with a quick grin. "But about what exactly?"

"Turns out, our guests don't actually care that they can't remember the entire weekend. People really do want to escape it all."

"And I couldn't be happier about that," Aunt Thelma leaned forward and imparted her thoughts.

Mayor Parrish cleared her throat into the mic. "Is this thing on?" She gave a nervous chuckle.

"I just heard from WNN, and our final numbers are in." The mayor looked like she was about to burst with excitement. "Silverlake raised over fifteen thousand dollars and is the winner of the Christmas Wish Contest!"

Cheers erupted all around us, but perhaps none were quite as loud as Sally's twin daughters.

"We did it!" Beatrice and Sabrina high-fived each other and then held hands and jumped around, spinning in a circle.

I couldn't help but be drawn into their excitement.

"What did you do?" Their mother asked, looking suspicious.

Sabrina and Beatrice immediately stopped

celebrating. The two shared a look before silently agreeing on something. "Promise you won't be mad?" Beatrice asked.

"I can promise I'll try," Sally replied.

The girls shared a look once more and must have decided that their mom's words were good enough because the following words out of Sabrina's mouth were, "We might have conjured a couple of dollars to donate."

"How many is a couple?" Sally said through clenched teeth. Dread washed over Sally's face as she appeared to mentally calculate how much money she would have to pay back. Every witch knew conjuring cash was illegal. It always came from somewhere. Money didn't magically appear from thin air.

Beatrice scrunched her nose. "I don't know. Do you know?" she directed her question to her sister.

"Beats me. I didn't keep track. We conjured it right to town hall."

Sally looked faint.

I rushed to her side. "It's okay. They didn't mean any harm."

"Yeah, mom, listen to Angelica. We didn't mean any harm," Sabrina said.

"And look how happy everyone is." Beatrice was right about that.

"What's going on?" Vance came over to join my side.

"I think we know who the Village Square pickpocket is." I motioned with my head to the twins, who were looking apprehensive.

Vance shook his head. "You have to be kidding me."

"They were only trying to win the contest," I explained.

"Well, it worked." Vance smiled at Sally.

"I have to let people know," she said as much to herself as to us.

Sally didn't wait a minute longer as she weaved her way through the crowd up to where Mayor Parrish stood. A second later, Sally held the mic in her hand.

"Hello, everyone." Her voice trembled. "Hi. Um, you see, I've just learned that my daughters may have taken money from quite a few of you. Turns out, they were conjuring cash to help win the contest." Sally looked down at the twins, who appeared sheepish as everyone's eyes settled upon them. "I wanted to let you know that I promise to pay you all back. If you could come up to me and let me know how much you're missing, I'll be sure to return it. Somehow." Sally took a deep breath and tried to smile. "Excuse me!" Annabelle called from the back. She waved her arms in the air to get everyone's attention before bending low to whisper in her dad's ear. She patted him on the shoulder and rushed forward, taking the microphone from Sally.

"That won't be necessary. My mom didn't leave a positive lasting legacy, and I'd like to do something about that. Not only will I gladly cover the missing money, but I'd also like to set up a music scholarship in my mother's name to be paid out every Christmas. Whether you need money for a new instrument or help to pay for music lessons, this is one way I can give back and make a difference. So, if you are missing money, let me know." Annabelle pointed to the center of her chest, "And stay tuned for more information about the scholarship. Thank you."

A fresh round of applause filled the park, followed by Mayor Parrish counting down from ten.

As the seconds ticked by and Wishing Well Park filled aglow, I leaned into Vance and realized that he would always be my home.

Next in the Series: Midnight at Mystic Inn

https://books2read.com/u/bPQ26Y

Stephanie Damore Complete Works

Mystic Inn Mysteries
Witchy Reservations
Eerie Check In
Spooked Solid
Untimely Departure
Midnight at Mystic Inn
Bewitch Break Inn
Potions, Poison, and Pumpkin Spice
Jingle Bells and Wedding Spells

. . .

Spirited Sweets Mysteries
Bittersweet Betrayal
Decadent Demise
Red Velvet Revenge
Sugared Suspect

Witch In Time
Better Witch Next Time
Play for Time
Time Will Tell

Beauty Secrets Series
Makeup & Murder
Kiss & Makeup
Eyeliner & Alibis
Pedicures & Prejudice
Beauty & Bloodshed
Charm & Deception

ABOUT THE AUTHOR

Stephanie Damore is a USA Today bestselling mystery author with a soft spot for magic and romance, too. She loves being on the beach, has a strong affinity for the color pink (especially in diamonds and champagne), and, not to brag, but chocolate and her are in a pretty serious relationship.

Her books are fun and fearless, and feature smart and sassy sleuths. If you love books with a dash of romance and twist of whodunit, you're going to love her work!

For information on new releases and fun giveaways, visit her Facebook group at https://www.facebook.com/stephdamoreauthor/

 facebook.com/stephdamoreauthor

 twitter.com/stephdamore

instagram.com/steph_damore_author

bookbub.com/profile/stephanie-damore